I0666353

Pirates of The Bahamas

Pirates of The Bahamas, Volume 1

Ronald Haines

Published by Haines Communications, 2022.

Table of Contents

Pirates of the Bahamas
by Ronald Haines

Prologue

The capture of Calico Jack Rackham at the end of 1720 essentially marked the end of the golden age of piracy in the Bahamas. While he was hanged, the two women pirates who were captured with him, Anne Bonny and Mary Read, were not.

Anne Bonny, only eighteen years old at the time, was released from jail into her father's custody and he took her back with him to Carolina in the American Colonies. One the journey home it was discovered that she was pregnant, but her father quickly married her off to Joseph Burleigh, a wealthy plantation owner before the baby was born. When Anne gave birth to a daughter she named her Mary, after her friend Mary Read, and Joseph Burleigh willingly raised her as his own. Now Anne Burleigh, and with her pirate past and the name Anne Bonny well behind her, Anne soon became acclimated to living the life of a lady and had an additional four daughters with Joseph.

The official records in Port Royal lists Mary Read as dying while giving birth to Jack Rackham's son, but that is simply the official story. The real story is that the prison authorities were bribed by friends of Rackham to let mother and baby escape, using her supposed death as a cover. Mary Read and her baby were taken back to their old base of operations in Isla de Pinos, an island just south of Cuba. She there named the boy Jack and raised him to follow in his father's footsteps.

In 1742 the War of Austrian Succession resulted in France and Spain being allied against England, opening up a new era of hostilities in the Caribbean. England was forced to concentrate her warships around the royal naval base in Jamaica, leaving the Bahamas unprotected. Once again, they became a haven for pirates.

Taking advantage of this opportunity, Mary and Jack Read moved north into the Bahamas and established a new base of operations on the island of Gran Baha. With treacherous reefs along the south coast most ships avoided this island, but with knowledge of passages through the reef it was perfect for the Reads and their compatriots. From this strategic position their pirate ships could intercept the lucrative merchant traffic between the American Colonies and the West Indies and return to safety without concerning themselves with being followed because no pursuer would venture near the reefs.

By the mid-1740s, Jack Read had was almost as well known a pirate as his father had been.

1. Mary Burleigh

1746 : South Carolina

IT WAS A CURSE OF PRIVILEGE that passions must be contained. Gentlemen, of course, had their outlets with their slaves, something everyone knew about but nobody discussed, but the ladies of South Carolina had no such recourse. Mary Burleigh wanted to know that passion with a man, but the gentlemen who came to call only saw her only as the daughter of a wealthy plantation owner in spite of her natural beauty. Men with sufficient societal rank to woo her would seemingly do so from the perspective of a good match and potential inheritance rather than having any actual interest in her as a woman. It was for that reason she remained single despite the fact she was perilously close to thirty years old. Her attitude was quite unique; two of her younger sisters were already married and a third betrothed. But, being the eldest of six children and with all of them being girls, Mary had always been the child closest to the operation of the plantation, so she reasoned that if the perfect gentleman failed to enter her life, she would be content to take over the family business when her father became unable, even if it carried with it the stigma of being an old maid. This was the steely resolve she presented to the world at large, but in the solitude of her dreams she continued to yearn for that elusive man; dreams in which she would never yield to a passionless marriage.

3

There was precedent for her hope in that her mother, Anne, had married later in life and had still had ample time to raise half a dozen children.

Mary had become quite proficient at plantation management, and her father already considered her indispensable. For the last two years she had accompanied him to Jamaica to sell the harvest, and this year she was to go on the trip alone while he remained to supervise the clearing of enough swampland to create two more rice fields. Mary was also to purchase two more planters while she was in Jamaica. Unlike field slaves, planters had the expertise of all aspects of rice farming, and their role was to supervise the production of an entire field with a dozen field slaves under them. Field slaves, right off the boat from Africa, were readily available being sold at auction in Charleston almost every week, but a good planter could only be bought in the Caribbean. And best planter slave market, by far, was in Kingston.

It was one of those perfect August days, and in spite of her mother's insistence that ladies should remain indoors so as to keep their skin pale, Mary was outside enjoying the summer breeze. It was far too sultry for her indoors. Besides, she liked having a light tan on her skin; it made her feel healthier. Bonnet in her hand, her long brunette hair danced around her shoulders while she watched the field slaves at work between the long rows of rice plants, which were now over four feet tall and almost ready to be harvested. Blithely lost in thoughts about her upcoming trip, she didn't hear Jethro approaching from behind until he announced rather loudly, "It gonna be a reel good crop this year, miz Mary, that be fur sure," in his sing-songy voice. He walked up and stood to her left, but respectfully, slightly behind her.

Mary looked over her shoulder and smiled at the grizzled planter. He'd always been old, yet she could swear that he hadn't changed a bit in the twenty something years that she had known him. She really liked Jethro; he was a constant on the plantation and probably the most knowledgeable person about growing rice in all of South Carolina, slave or free man.

"Massa tells me y'all be off ta Kingston by yerseff ta sell the crop and ta buy me another two planters." Jethro was so well trusted that Mary's father had the other planters report to him. It always amused Mary how Jethro felt his supervisory role somehow elevated him to speak as if the other slaves were his; as if this position made him something more than a slave himself. Jethro's abilities were certainly respected, and he was always treated well by the family, but he was still just property.

"That's correct, Jethro. This is to be my opportunity to demonstrate how capable I am."

"Ah, you reelly be the son your father never had, miz Mary," he said proudly while flashing a full set of ivory teeth, but then thoughtfully doused his contagious smile, "But don't cha worry 'bout travelin' by ship?"

"Not at all; it's still quite too early in the year to be concerned about hurricanes."

"'tain't hurricanes I be talking about, miz Mary. It be pirates."

"Oh, there's no need to worry on that account, Jethro." Mary responded, both hands clasping her bonnet as she turned to face him. "French and Spanish ships offer far superior plunder than colonial merchants, so any pirates between here and Jamaica have undoubtedly turned privateer since the war began. They'll all be somewhere off in the southern Caribbean flying the king's colors." She smiled knowingly, which added a slight blush to her delicately tanned cheeks. "I'll warrant there isn't a pirate left to be found in the whole of the Bahamas."

The rice was harvested the next week, and by mid-September it had been threshed, polished, and was earnestly being loaded onto carts to be taken to the docks. Mary's father, Joseph Burleigh, accompanied Mary to Charleston in order to confer with the captain before they left. An astute businessman, Joseph owned a merchant vessel, *The Anne*, a two mast snow which he had named after Mary's mother. Ship ownership enabled him to sell the harvest at a much higher price directly in the Jamaica market and net double over what he would have received by simply selling his rice to a wholesaler at the Charleston dock, a practice that was more the norm for other plantation owners.

As he and Mary walked along the pier to where the ship was moored, Joseph called out, "Captain Fordham," to a tall, burly man sporting full grey sideburns under a black tricorn hat who was overseeing the loading of *The Anne*. "How goes it?"

"We're well on schedule, Mister Burleigh," Captain Fordham boomed back. It made sense that a sea captain would have a loud voice. "And we'll be under weigh with tomorrow's high tide." He shook hands with Joseph and turned his voice down to conversational volume. "I received your note that only your daughter will be coming to Kingston this year; I shall miss playing cards with you."

"And I with you, Captain, but I suspect you may find Mary here to be a worthy opponent."

"Then I'll look forward to a new challenge." Captain Fordham smiled at Mary. "Come aboard, Miss Burleigh, and let's get you settled. Since your father's not sailing with us, you'll be having the owner's cabin." He turned to Joseph. "The three of us can sit at the table in there and finalize the details for the trip."

The owner's cabin on *The Anne* was below deck directly beneath the captain's cabin and occupied the entire width of the stern. It was as big as Mary's bedroom at home, and in addition to a bed, two armchairs and chests of drawers, there was a table with four chairs in the middle which the three of them sat down at.

"Now, Mary," Joseph began. "Captain Fordham has been making trading runs for us for over twenty years, so while you have the authority to buy and sell, I want him to accompany you to the markets and you are to take his counsel to heart. I always do, and his advice has always been spot on."

"I'd be most grateful, captain," Mary nodded eagerly in agreement. It was a relief to have his expertise to accompany her first solo.

The conversation continued but was interrupted by the arrival of a boy, perhaps eleven years old, who was noisily dragging a wooden chest behind him. "Forgive the interruption," he gasped when he realized the cabin was occupied. "I was bringing Miss Burleigh's chest down, and didn't know anyone was here."

"It's quite all right," Captain Fordham said in a soothing voice. "Come in and meet the owners of the ship." He placed his left hand reassuringly on the boy's right shoulder. "This is James," he explained. "James is the youngest son of the governor. This is to be his first time at sea, and he'll be making the journey with us as cabin boy."

"It's an honor to meet both of you." James bowed slightly before backing away and scurrying off down the hallway.

"Why do you not have slaves perform cabin boy duties, captain?" Mary tightened her eyebrows. "Running errands seems rather menial for a person of rank."

"The only slaves you'll ever find on my ship will be in the cargo hold, Miss Mary, and being assistant to a ship's captain is far from menial." The captain's tone was a combination of explanation with a polite underlay of admonishment. "Time as a cabin boy is the perfect indoctrination to the running of an entire vessel, and it serves to prepare a lad to become a junior officer if he so desires."

"My apologies, sir." Mary was contrite.

"None needed." Captain Fordham's sideburns twitched upwards in a rather comical fashion. "In fact, please forgive me my overenthusiastic outburst regarding slaves.

The meeting continued for another fifteen minutes ending with Captain Fordham's, "And don't you worry, Mister Burleigh; Miss Mary will be quite safe."

Mary awoke the next morning to the sounds of activity throughout the ship, and dressing quickly, she was soon up on deck to watch the crew prepare for departure. Her father who had stayed on board in order to see her off, was standing next to the captain amidships, and as she approached them James appeared and gave her a mug of hot tea while Captain Fordham greeted her with a vociferous, "Good morning Miss Mary."

Mary theorized that whenever the captain was on deck he wanted the entire crew to hear him.

"We'll be breakfasting once we're under weigh," he continued.

"Then I'd best go ashore and leave you to it," Mary's father said, and after exchanging hugs with his daughter, he sauntered down the gangplank. It was pulled aboard the instant he stepped onto land.

Mary looked up into the rigging where a dozen crewmen were crawling around like so many spiders in a giant web, getting into position to untie the thick ropes that were holding the sails in tidy bundles. On the main deck the dock lines were furiously being reeled in. It was all so exciting. The crew pulled the jib halyards to unfurl the small sails around the bowsprit, and *The Anne* responded by immediately catching the light offshore breeze and moving away from the dock and into Charleston harbor. Mary waved at her father on shore for just long enough to be polite, and then hurried to the bow as the crew released the six mainsails from the crosspars. *The Anne* rapidly picked up speed as the sails filled with wind and took shape. They were off.

2. Pirates

The trip to Jamaica had been very profitable, and Mary was feeling particularly proud of herself. Buyers in Kingston were eager to purchase rice, and the entire cargo was snapped up within the first day of *The Anne's* arrival. Her holds were now loaded with barrels of rum, molasses, sugar and ginger, and the ship was heading back to South Carolina.

Mary had also successfully purchased two buck planters from the slave market for "an excellent price" according to Captain Fordham, and the remainder of the proceeds had been converted into ambergris, which was kept in a drawer in the captain's cabin. Easily overlooked as mere rocks or chunks of clay, ambergris was a much safer medium to carry than gold and would also return a tidy profit when sold back in Charleston.

To avoid Spanish warships they returned by sailing north along the Windward Passage just west of Hispaniola rather than risking the faster route around Cuba. A snow could sail closer to the wind than a frigate, so if an enemy ship had been sighted *The Anne* would most likely be able to outrun it on that tack. All the same, the first few days out of Kingston had been tense with double lookouts posted. But yesterday they had entered the safety of the waters around the British Bahamas, and they were now picking up speed with the wind behind them as they made their way through the Northwest Providence Channel, heading for the Florida Straits.

Mary was on deck with Jermy and Willum, her two newly acquired slaves. The captain had reluctantly agreed to allow them to be let out of the hold for two hours per day, provided they remained under Mary's constant supervision while they were unshackled.

"So you both worked on the same plantation?" Other than the fact they were experienced planters Mary knew little about them.

"Yessum, Miz Mary," Willum responded. "Massa Smith had five of us planters, but when crops switched ta sugar cane we wuz too valuable to work fields, an' so we got sold. Massa got six workers each fur Jermy and me."

"Well, we will certainly put your expertise to use, and you'll be treated well. Our plantation works on a task basis, so once your work is done for the day the remainder of it is your own time."

"Thank you, miz," Jermy nodded as he spoke. "You works all of the daylight time in da cane fields."

"Then I imagine you are both very appreciative that it was me that purchased you."

"Yez, miz," they chimed in unison.

Once Willum and Jermy were secured again in the hold, Mary sought out Captain Fordham or the foredeck. "I notice that we seem to be changing course quite often captain," she asked. "Is everything all right?"

"Oh, everything's fine, Miss Mary," he responded while studying the clouds. "It's just that the wind has shifted to the northwest, and so we have to tack back and forth now to make any decent headway." He turned his gaze back down from the sky and smiled at her. "Although these winds usually mean we're about to get rain too. The next couple of days might be a bit rough weather wise."

"What's that?" Mary suddenly interrupted him and pointed towards a white object that had just appeared on the horizon. As the captain trained his spyglass on it, the watch in the crow's nest called out, "Ship ahoy, twenty degrees off the starboard bow," from high in the mast above them.

"Curious," Captain Fordham muttered, but before Mary could ask what was going on, he spun around and began barking out orders. "All hands make ready to tack. Helm, take us to seventy five degrees."

"What is it, captain?" Mary asked anxiously as *The Anne* changed course and Captain Fordham once again raised his glass to study the other ship.

"I'm not completely sure," he said, focusing the lens back and forth. "It's a sloop, but she's not flying any flags and isn't in any merchant shipping lane. It's a good rule of thumb to steer clear of any ship you can't identify. If she holds course, she'll pass well clear of us, though, and we can safely maintain this heading until we sight Andros."

Mary sensed there was more to it than the captain was letting on and wanted to pressure him about why he was being so cautious, but that became clear when he suddenly blurted out, "Damn it," as the sloop turned south on an intercept course. "They've raised the Skull and Cutlasses. It's *The Avenger*."

"You mean they're pirates?" Mary's voice was suddenly reduced to a whisper.

"Aye, and the captain of that ship is Jack Read, the son of Calico Jack Rackham." Captain Fordham's right hand, still clutching the spyglass, dropped to his side and he turned directly at Mary. "That's what gives him the right to fly his father's flag."

"May I take a look?" Mary asked meekly.

The captain handed her the spyglass, and she gasped when she saw the huge black flag fluttering from the stern. "Can we outrun them?"

"She's faster than us on all points of sail except downwind, Miss Mary," Captain Fordham said as he took the spyglass back. "But with this northwesterly, downwind will drive us right onto the Bahamian reefs." He looked again through the spyglass at the Avenger bearing fast on their position. "They're going to catch us within the hour and there's naught we can do about it."

"So what will you do, captain? You are going to fight, aren't you?"

"You don't fight pirates, miss. Best way to stay alive is to let them come aboard without fuss. Hopefully, all they'll want is the cargo."

"What do you mean, hopefully?"

"Well, sometimes a pirate captain will take the ship, too, if he takes a fancy to it."

Mary was incredulous when she began to realize that her father's ship and cargo was about to simply be turned over to pirates. Captain Fordham ignored her continuing protests, and half an hour later the Avenger fired a shot across *The Anne's* bow. The cannon ball splashed into the sea fifty feet to the port side. "Heave to and prepare to be boarded," Captain Fordham yelled out to the crew. "James?"

"Yes, sir." James was suddenly as his side.

"Take Miss Burleigh below and lock her in her cabin." The captain then turned back to Mary. "I want you to hide in there. Don't let them see you. If we don't provoke them, there's hope they'll just take the cargo and let the ship and crew go."

Mary fumed as James locked her cabin door. She'd have Captain Burleigh stripped of his command for cowardice as soon as she could tell her father about this. As for her, she was going to be ready to confront a pirate. Trembling, she removed a wooden box from the top drawer and took out a pistol. She had never used one before but loading it was relatively straightforward, and after tamping down the barrel with the rod, she cocked the weapon and crouched down beside the bed. With the shutters closed the room was dark, so unless someone was to actually come in to search the room, she most likely wouldn't be seen in there and could lay in wait to surprise them.

Mary remained motionless for what must have been the biggest part of an hour while she listened to all sorts of shouts and crashes coming from the rest of the ship. She held her breath and felt like her heart was about to leap out of her chest at one point when the door rattled as someone tried to open it, but they didn't force it and moved on. Things had quieted down now, and it sounded like people were simply talking up on deck. Had the pirates left? She crept towards the door, pistol still in hand, hoping that position would let her hear more clearly what might be happening above. She was halfway to the door when it suddenly burst open. The glaring light temporarily blinded her dark accustomed eyes, and the pistol she was holding fired into the ceiling as the pirate grabbed her right wrist. "Be careful with that, lass," he said teasingly. "You might hurt somebody."

"Unhand me," Mary screamed at him. "Just who do you think you are?"

"My name is Jack Read, but you can call me captain." He laughed as Mary struggled fruitlessly to free her wrist from his strong grip. "We have a feisty one here, lads," he announced as he dragged her effortlessly out of the cabin and up the stairway. In the light she could see he was a man about her own age, and unlike *The Anne's* captain, was quite tall and fit looking.

"You told me the owner wasn't aboard, Captain, and yet look what I found in the owner's cabin." The pirate pulled Mary across the deck and handed her off to two men who each took hold of one of her arms. She furiously looked around for assistance, but *The Anne's* crew was grouped together on the aft deck, surrounded by a half dozen pirates with their cutlasses drawn. The rest of the pirates were taking barrels from the hold and loading them into nets, which were then being swung over to the pirate ship.

"I'm the owner's daughter so you'd better release me if you know what's good for you."

"Are you now?" Jack Read turned and grinned at her. "Then you clearly meant to say ransom not release. You're an item of value, so just like the rest of the cargo, you'll be coming with us."

"I beseech you, Captain Read," Captain Burleigh began, but the pirate captain raised his right hand to silence him. Unlike the other pirates who were wearing ordinary seaman's clothing, Captain Read was dressed like a gentleman with a blue silk jacket and well fitted trousers, yet his open necked shirt looked to be of ordinary cotton. His clean shaven face, which Mary could not help staring at because it was so annoyingly handsome, was rugged and deeply tanned, almost the color of his leather hat, which held his long, dark hair in place. It was sticking out in a tail behind it. He looked back at Mary. "What's your name?" he asked her.

"My name is Mary Burleigh," she snorted out indignantly. "And my father will have you hanged for this."

"Quartermaster," Captain Read called out without acknowledging Mary's threat. "Determine what ransom Mister Burleigh can handle for his daughter and write up a note for me to sign." He turned to Captain Fordham. "I'm sure, that if I let your ship continue on its way, you'll be kind enough to deliver my note to him. Yes?"

When the cargo had been transferred, the remaining pirates came back up from *The Anne's* hold. Mary was horrified to see Jermy and Willum were walking free amongst them.

"Captain Read," she shouted as loud as she could in order to get his attention. "I can understand why you're stealing our rum, but what need does a pirate ship have of slaves?"

"Absolutely none, Miss Burleigh. Were you by chance referring to these two able bodied men who are voluntarily joining my crew?"

"They can't voluntarily do anything, they belong to me."

The entire pirate crew burst into laughter.

"In my world no person has the right to own another, and you are in my world now." He spoke with unquestioning authority. "So, if you don't mind, would you please be quiet; I'm trying to conduct business here."

Mary began to shriek about how she was a lady and deserved to be treated with respect, but Captain Read just sighed and addressed the men who were holding her. "Get this banshee over to the Avenger and secure her in the brig so I don't have to listen to her anymore," he said.

Mary was tossed backwards into a net, which quickly closed around her as it was hauled up and swung across to the pirate ship. This brute of a captain might dress like a gentleman, but his lack of respect for a lady of position clearly labeled him as a lout. The least he could have done was look at her while she was being manhandled away to make sure she made it across safely. She stared at him through the rope netting, and the unthinkable finally dawned on her. He didn't care who she was. Mary was used to men always paying deference to her, but to this pirate captain she was just a piece of cargo.

By the time she was unceremoniously unloaded onto the deck of the Avenger, this harsh realization had reduced Mary into becoming dazed and passive. She offered no resistance when two men escorted her below and locked her in a small dark room in the bowels of the pirate ship. She sank down onto a pile of straw in the corner of the room in disbelief about what was happening to her and looked up at the only source of light, a 2 foot square opening high on the door, that was fortified with iron bars.

3. Captive and Auctioned

Mary was awakened by the creaking of the opening door, but before she could focus her eyes, it had closed again, and there was now a bucket of water and a plate of food on the floor next to it. "Hello?" she called out, but there was no reply. She quickly scrambled to her feet and peered through the bars at what appeared to be a general storage area, but as far as she could tell there were no people there. "Hello?" she repeated, this time a little quieter. The gentle rocking told her that the ship was under sail, and diffuse light beams streaming into the hold indicated it was daytime, but that was all she knew. She reached into the bucket, scooped water into her hand, and after gingerly tasting it to determine it was fresh, knelt down next to it and scooped up several handfuls to drink, then washed her face. Her initial thought was not to eat as a display of protest, but she was hungry. The food was a piece of hardtack which broke in half easily, indicating it was quite fresh, and a firm orange. This ship could not have been at sea for more than a week.

She sat with her back against the wall and slowly ate the food while straining her ears, but it was quite some time before Mary heard activity at all outside. When she finally did, she instantly jumped to her feet and brushed the straw from her dress as the door opened.

One of the pirate crew stepped halfway inside. "Quartermaster says you're to be allowed on deck," he told her. "You ready?"

"Indeed I am," she blurted out belligerently. "I have been detained in here quite long enough, thank you."

"Well then," the pirate was taken aback. "We'd better go, 'adn't we?"

"And you can tell your captain that I wish to speak with him."

"Sorry miss, but you'll have to take that up with the quartermaster."

Mary squinted when she was led out into the midday light and shaded her eyes with her right hand as the pirate delivered her to the aft deck where the quartermaster was waiting. He was tall, like the captain, but was an older man and had a scraggly graying beard.

"Good day, Miss Burleigh. I trust you slept well?"

"Well enough," Mary answered brusquely.

"You're to be our guest on board the Avenger for another month or so before we head back to home base," he told her. "And then you'll be staying there 'til we exchange you for your ransom."

"And will I be expected to spend this month in that horrid little room you had me locked in?"

"Certainly not," the quartermaster's teeth shone through his beard and he broke into a hearty guffaw. "Why, I suspect you'll be finding yourself in a regular cabin before the day is out." He massaged his chin with his right hand and leered at her. "Right as soon as you're married."

"What!"

"It's custom. If any member of the crew is willing to put his share of the ransom money back into the pot he can have you until you're ransomed off, and you will get to stay in a cabin with him 'til then. It's just a temporary marriage."

"It's rape."

"Depends on how you look at it, don't it? We like to call it marriage so as not to sound so offensive."

Mary clenched her teeth and glared directly into his face.

"Of course, if more than one of the crew takes a fancy to you, then we have an auction and you go to the highest bidder."

"I doubt you'll get too many bidders for this one, quartermaster." Captain Read said as he stepped up onto the aft deck. "We haven't been back at sea that long, and she is a bit scrawny."

Mary had been so focused on the quartermaster that she hadn't noticed the pirate captain approaching them. She was so flabbergasted by his insult that she completely forgot the well-rehearsed tirade that she had planned to lash out at him. Clearly, it would have done no good anyway. As a lady, she was used to men being courteous, even fawning up to her. But here, for the first time in her life, was a man who was completely dismissive to her station.

"I dare say that Jermy or Willum might be interested, though," the captain continued. "And that would be sort of equitable like."

"Aye, it would be at that, captain," the quartermaster nodded thoughtfully. "But they joined the crew after the raid where we took her, so they're not entitled to a share."

"Well, Miss Burleigh," the captain finally spoke directly to her. "I imagine you'll at least be thankful for that."

"What do you mean by scrawny?" It was the first thing she could think of to say. It was strange that how the captain looked at her seemed more important than the prospect of being forcibly ravaged. She might have been slender, but she always considered herself well-proportioned and was quite aware of the effect she had on the gentlemen of South Carolina. "Perhaps you are simply not accustomed to being in the presence of a real lady."

"Perhaps not, 'your ladyship,'" he feigned a slight bow. "But most of the men on this ship would prefer a woman to a lady; one with a bit more meat on her bones." He visually scanned her from waist to eyes. "And, shall we say, a fuller bodice."

"I'll have you know..." Mary began indignantly, then caught herself and took a deep breath. "Captain," she said calmly. "May I appeal to your good nature to allow me to preserve my honor while I am your captive?"

"And deprive the men of their sport? They wouldn't consider me a very good captain then, would they? Besides, distribution of the spoils is the up to the quartermaster."

"Then make me a member of your crew. As captain you can do that, can't you?"

"I could," Captain Read chuckled. "But what skills could you bring to benefit the ship?"

"I thought you just needed bodies to do work. What skills did Jermy and Willum offer?"

"Jermy plays a flute, and the men are mighty fond of music. And Willum, Willum is a striker."

"A what?"

"A striker's a hunter who catches meat ashore and fish and turtles while we're at sea. The cook was well pleased to have him aboard, and I sincerely doubt that you could do the same. So I ask you again, Miss Burleigh, what could you possibly offer, other than the wifely services that the crew have you pegged for?"

"You don't have a cabin boy, do you?" She suddenly remembered the role of James on *The Anne*. "Think about it, captain; an assistant. Someone to run your errands, fetch your food..."

"Enough," Captain Read raised his hand and waved it in the air as he walked away laughing loudly.

It was dusk when the pirates collected on the main deck, and the quartermaster paraded Mary out in front of them. She stood tall and proud as if she was daring any man to try to take her. Her height-of-fashion blue dress, when compared to the simple attire of this crew, supported her sense of superiority over them. She was also aware that Captain Read was studying her, but she refused to acknowledge his attention and simply stared above the heads of the assembled crewmen.

"All right you lot," the quartermaster bellowed as he addressed the crowd. "Any man here who wants to trade his share of the ransom for time with this woman, step forward."

Mary refused to as much as flinch as three men stepped forward, and all the pirates gleefully shouted, "Auction," in loud unison.

"Wait, I've a better idea." It was Captain Read stepping between Mary and the men. "This woman's strength of character impresses me, and it would be a shame to not put that to good use. I bid the entire captain's share of the ransom to have her as my assistant until she is to be returned."

"Will that be assistant, but not wife, captain?" The quartermaster asked quizzically as the pirates burst into raucous laughter.

"Aye, quartermaster; she'll be my cabin girl, and in that capacity, will also be a respected member of this ship's crew." He turned to Mary and smiled at her. "I believe she possesses the perfect temperament for dealing with the likes of you 'gentlemen.'"

"Done!" The quartermaster grinned and dismissed the assembly. "Shall I assign her to a cabin, or will you want her bunked in with you, captain?"

"Give her the small cabin next to mine, quartermaster."

"Thank you, captain," Mary said, unable to contain her genuine relief.

"I was also helping my crew, Miss Burleigh. Most of these men are already married, and their wives would give them holy hell if they found out their husbands had gone for a piece of strumpet instead of bringing their earnings home." Captain Read smirked at the quartermaster, who was clearly amused by what he had just said, but continued to speak to Mary. "Join me in my cabin in an hour, and we will discuss your duties over dinner." He then quickly disappeared towards the stern of the ship.

"You've really caught the captain's attention, young lady." The quartermaster spoke sincerely. "I never would have believed Captain Jack to be willing to give up his shares of ransom just to keep a captive from being married to one of the crew."

"Is the captain married?" She felt a slight blush as she wondered why she had even asked that question.

"Captain Jack? No, never has the right girl for him ever come along. Doubt that one ever will."

An hour later, Mary was eating turtle stew and freshly baked bread in Captain Jack's well-appointed cabin. The mahogany furniture, rich velvet bed curtains and cypress paneling would have been the envy of many a plantation owner. The man himself had changed into a purple silk shirt. He certainly enjoyed his luxuries. Jack was a man with passion in his life. He was also the well-respected captain of a ship, which put him in the same league as gentlemen ashore. She had never imagined that one so disconnected from the life she had always known could be so captivating for her, yet here she was enjoying dinner with him.

"Now, while it is true that we pirates like our rum, I find wine much more palatable at dinner," he said as he refilled their goblets. "Don't you?"

"I've never tasted rum," Mary confessed.

"I'm sure we can remedy that in the time you're aboard. If you like, that is."

They finished off their meal with mangoes that Jack deftly opened and cubed with his dagger, providing them with bite sized chunks on small plates to be eaten delicately with a fork rather than the messy alternative of biting into the whole fruit.

"Now then," Jack said. "Your duties as cabin girl will first consist of bringing my meals here from the galley, and you and I will take our evening meal together right here." He tapped on the table top. "You'll also run messages between me and the officers during the day. You've already met the quartermaster. Tomorrow you'll meet the other two officers, bosun and shipmaster, and I'll have each of them explain what it is that they do and show you around the ship. You'd better be a quick learner."

"I'm quite confident that you will find me to be a most capable assistant, captain."

"Splendid! Since you're my cabin girl, I'll be calling you by your first name. Mary, isn't it?"

"Yes, captain; it is."

"The rest of my crew calls me captain, Mary, but you will call me sir."

"Yes, sir," Mary couldn't contain a demure smile as she responded. She liked that, it seemed right. "How long will I be in your service, sir?" she asked.

"In order to give your father time to pull the ransom together, we set the exchange to be in early December, so you'll be with us for another couple of months."

"I see." Mary nodded slowly, then quietly added, "And what of my honor and dignity during that time?"

"Since you're in service to me, your honor will be quite safe from the crew." Jack drained his goblet and smirked. "Your dignity is entirely up to you."

"Thank you, sir."

"You won't want to be wearing that dress any more while you're aboard, though. It's not very well suited to running around the ship."

"Do you want me to take it off, sir?" The words fell out of Mary's mouth without thought. As a lady, she should have reacted with shock or embarrassment at such an utterance. Instead, her mouth just wrinkled demurely and she felt a light blushing in her cheeks.

Jack apparently failed to pick up on any potential innuendo, however. "You must be tired," he told her. "I'll have shirt and trousers for you to wear tomorrow delivered to your cabin." Was he being gallant, or just indifferent?

"That is very kind of you, sir. It has been quite a day."

"Then I shall see you in the morning. Goodnight, Mary."

"Damn," Mary thought to herself as she went to her cabin. Jack had all of the qualities she dreamed of in a man, but he clearly was not looking at her as a woman. She had certainly implied her interest in him. Was she too scrawny for him? She lay bewildered on the bed until she fell asleep with the realization that, perhaps, this pirate captain really was a gentleman.

4. Cabin Girl

Within days Mary knew her way around *The Avenger* and had learned the names of all 27 men aboard. She was on a first name basis with everybody except the officers, whom she referred to by their title as did the rest of the crew. Each day had a set routine for her. First thing in the morning she met with the bosun for his state-of-the-ship report, and then delivered it to the captain when she took him his breakfast. Captain Jack would then give her the day's headings to take to the shipmaster, while he remained in his cabin and ate. For the rest of the day she ran messages between the officers when called on, but most of her time was her own and she found she enjoyed exploring the ship and talking to the crew, who readily accepted her as one of them.

The person she spoke to the most was Andy, the ships cook. He was a pirate who had served aboard various ships for almost thirty years. His leg had been blown off in battle over a decade ago, but he chose to spend the rest of his life at sea rather than retire as a landlubber. It was just as well because, with his fondness for rum, his pension had long been spent. He was recruited as a cook by Captain Jack on his first command, and over the years Andy had become quite proficient with his culinary skills. Mary enjoyed chatting with him when she picked up Jack's meals, and it soon became clear to her that Andy seemed to know almost everything about everybody.

Mary admired the way Jack ran the ship and the culture of democracy aboard. People's jobs were based on their skills and the officers were elected by the crew as the best men to serve in their particular position. She also learned that everyone on board, be they cook, gunner or officer, received an equal share of whatever profit the ship brought in with the only two exceptions being the quartermaster, who received one and a half shares, and the captain receiving two. It was this sense of fairness that was often the topic of discussion at their evening meal.

"Tell me, Mary." Jack asked that evening. "Now that you've been part of the crew for more than a week, has it changed your attitude towards slavery?"

"I admit that recognizing inherent freedom of each person is admirable, sir, but surely that can only apply in the unique environment of your ship. Slavery is the backbone of the economics of the world at large. Without it, there would be no rice crops, no plantations, and no civilization as we know it."

"What if you paid them wages as free men?"

"But then there wouldn't be enough for the..." her voice trailed off.

"Life of luxury you extort from the lives of your slaves?" Jack eyes lit with satisfaction as his finishing her sentence underscored his argument.

Mary had no verbal response; mixed thoughts were now running rampant in her head. She thought of Jethro and how much his extensive skills would be worth in a free market; paying fair wages to him and the other slaves would most certainly bankrupt the family. Yet she had gotten to know Jermy and Willum as human beings this past week, and in her heart, she knew that Jack was right.

"They call us criminals," Jack continued, "But isn't the money we're relieving from families like yours come by through an even greater, moral, criminality?"

Mary was visibly taken aback as the hypocrisy of the only life she had ever known was laid out before her. How was she ever going to be comfortable again living that way when she was back home? She smiled adoringly at Jack, and without realizing it, her hand slid across the table towards him.

"But enough of my philosophizing," Jack said abruptly, quickly rising from the table and pretending not to notice Mary's hand. "You must be tired, Mary."

"Yes, sir," she responded quietly. She diverted her hand towards her glass of wine, picked it up and finished it.

"You'd better be careful not to fall too hard for Captain Jack, Mary," Andy told her when she was picking up breakfast the next morning. Was she really that transparent?

"Tell me, Andy," Mary asked. "Sometimes when I'm talking to the captain I feel like he really likes me, but then he always pulls away when he realizes he is sending me that signal." Mary shrugged. "What do you make of that?"

"Ah, it's like this." Andy's head slowly nodded as he attended to the pot on the stove. "I suppose the best way to put it is that our Captain Jack has a dread fear of love." Andy smiled at Mary's confusion. "His father, Calico Jack, got killed because of it, you see. If he hadn't let love guide his actions he might have lived or at least he would have died a noble death instead of with his head in a noose. Captain Jack wants to make sure all of his decisions come from his head and not his heart. Those are good qualities in a captain, the crew trusts him for it, but it does condemn him to a lonely life." Andy handed the tray to Mary. "So if you two really are getting feelings for each other, it's gonna be best for you both when you're off this ship and back at your rightful home."

Mary languished thoughtfully amidships at the rail looking aimlessly out to sea for the remainder of the morning, and would probably have stayed like that all day but was jarred by a shout of, "Sail ahoy, twenty degrees to port," from up in the rigging. She rushed to the bow and stood next to the master of the watch as he raised his spyglass. "What is it?" she asked.

"It's a brigantine," he responded, slowly closing the spyglass. "Go rouse the captain, Mary. Tell him there's a prize to be had."

The news caused Jack to immediately spring into action. As soon as he had donned his blue silk jacket, he grabbed his tan tricorn hat and walked briskly to the bow with Mary in tow. He pushed his hat ceremonially onto his head, and the master of the watch handed him the spyglass. Jack's face beamed as he focused on the merchant vessel. "Helm," he called out. "Put us on a beat bearing directly at the enemy. Bosun, break out cutlasses and two pistols for every man, and one pistol for the cabin girl." He folded the spyglass and swung around. "Quartermaster,"

"Yes, captain."

"Have your boarding party at the ready."

"Aye aye, captain," the quartermaster responded and disappeared amidships.

Jack continued barking out orders. "Gun crews, prepare for action. Jermy, give us a lively tune if you will. And Mary,"

"Yes, sir?"

"Stay close."

The Avenger was suddenly crashing through the waves, heeling back and forth between fifteen and twenty degrees while bearing down directly at their quarry. Jack moved to the back rail of the foredeck and addressed the crew. "We're closing in on a merchant brigantine of at least a hundred tons. A ship of this size is bound to be carrying worthy booty indeed, eh lads?"

The pirates cheered, temporarily downing out Jermy's furious flute.

"We might even take her as a prize so let's try and keep her intact. Gunners, if she does make a run for it, just take down the rigging." Jack drew his sword and held it above his head as the bosun handed Mary a pistol. "Are you ready, lads?" Jack shouted feverishly.

"Ready," was the chorus reply, followed by what could only be described as a semblance of a flute inspired song from the pirate crew as they boisterously swarmed into attack position.

"Raise the Skull and Cutlasses and open the gun ports. Gun number one, give her a warning shot." Jack rushed to the prow of the ship and as soon as the cannon fired he called out to the brigantine to surrender, his right hand holding his sword above his head and his left holding onto the deck gun. The brigantine immediately headed into the wind to stop, its sails instantly luffing, and as soon as *The Avenger* was alongside it the quartermaster and his boarding crew swarmed aboard. Mary, amazed at the precision, simply stood at Jack's side and cradled the unloaded pistol she had been given while they watched the action. After about fifteen minutes Tom swung back aboard and reported to Jack.

"Quartermaster says all secure, captain."

"Thank you, Tom. Mary, you stay here."

Jack boarded the brigantine, and Mary watched him through the spyglass as he spoke to the ship's captain. She smiled as she recalled the same incident on *The Anne* and knew what was transpiring. It was still so recent, and yet, in her memory of it, it felt like it had happened years ago. Just as she remembered, though, Jack was magnificent.

The brigantine's holds were full of flour, sugar and cotton, more cargo than *The Avenger* could take on, so she was taken as a prize. The quartermaster took command of her, taking six men from *The Avenger* with him. The rest of his crew was made up of recruits from the captured vessel, those sailors who elected to join the pirate band in return for a share of the spoils for their service. The merchant's captain, officers, and crew who remained loyal to them were taken prisoner and locked in the ship's hold. They would be put into boats a few miles from a friendly shore so they could easily row in. With Jack as captain, no one who surrendered to *The Avenger* had ever been killed, and Jack had never lost a crewmember.

Jack wasn't in his cabin when Mary delivered dinner that night, and since this was the first time she had ever been alone in his cabin, she quickly succumbed to the temptation to look around after she had set the table. She picked up his leather tricorn and gingerly tried in on, and noticing a full length mirror to the side of the bed began toying with Jack's hat in different poses. Having not had access to a mirror since she had been on board, she realized in the reflection that the clothing she wore made her look androgynous. "Hmm," she preened, pulling the shirt tightly from behind hoping to emphasize her shape. "Deficient in the bodice, am I?" she muttered, paraphrasing what Jack had said to her when she was first aboard. "The men like a little meat, do they?" Caught up in the moment, Mary took her shirt off and tossed it on the bed, then studied her breasts in the mirror. Placing a hand beneath each of them she pushed them up in an attempt to make them look fuller. "What about these?" she puffed proudly to herself.

Jack's reply, "I think they're very nice indeed," shocked her. Her hands instinctively slid up to cover her nipples as she gasped. How long had he been there? But, rather than reach for her shirt, she stood tall, her hands still covering her breasts, and turned to face him. "Please tell me, sir," she asked cautiously, her eyes hopeful, "Do you still find me to be inadequate as a woman?" Her lips trembled, flinching between a contained lack of expression and a questioning smile. She slowly slid her hands down her body to reveal her excited nipples which resembled stout stiff stems adorning ripe pears.

"I find you to be perfect, Mary." Jack took a step closer to her, "And eminently desirable."

Breathing heavily, Mary rushed to him and flung her arms around his neck, knocking the hat from her head. "Then take me," she whispered while squeezing him tightly. "Take me now."

The passion with which Jack enveloped Mary in his arms and nuzzled hot breath into her hair dispelled all previous pretense of his sexual indifference towards her. His mouth slid past her left ear to the side of her neck as he leaned her against his powerful left arm and then traced a line back up the side of her neck and under her chin with the tip of his tongue, coaxing her head to lean back. Mary's eyes closed as Jack's mouth descended onto hers in a forceful, open mouthed kiss while his right hand ravaged her left breast. She would surely have collapsed to the floor if Jack hadn't mercifully slid his right arm under her knees and scooped her up. He carried her to the bed and laid her on the sheets, his eyes burning into hers while he quickly threw his clothing onto the floor, and then unceremoniously stripped Mary's pants from her in a single movement.

In an instant he was on top of her; her legs forced up and held apart by his arms while his hands firmly pinned her wrists to the bed. Jack pushed his tongue into Mary's gasping mouth and simultaneously thrust his cock between her engorged labia lips and into her soaked vagina. His hips commenced with a rhythmical in and out while he held her in that position, a rhythm that quickly increased in intensity until it reached the fury of a staccato after only a few minutes. Both of their bodies pulsing, Jack slid his hands downwards, caressing her arms and torso while continuing his fevered pounding, and freed her legs before positioning her hands above her head. He slid his mouth from hers to permit release of her scream of ecstasy while he collapsed onto her and became motionless, satiated and soaked with sweat.

Mary woke first the next morning but remained quite still so she could watch Jack sleep. She had committed the sin of spending the night with a man to whom she was not married. But rather than any feelings of guilt, she felt only elation. Her married sisters had told her of the pleasures of being with a man, but the closed mouth pecks and ritualistic intercourse they had described was nothing like she had just experienced. A conventional gentleman would never have behaved in that way with a lady; only a slave girl would have been treated in the manner that Jack did with her. Mary smiled at her good fortune that Jack was a man who didn't hold to convention and allowed her to experience a passion she could have never have known at home. Yet in a way that might have seemed almost contradictory, for Jack had spent the remainder of the night holding her in tender embrace. "You're quite a man, Jack Read," she said under her breath. She then leaned over to kiss his eyes awake and whispered to him, "I'll be right back with your breakfast."

5. Harbour Island

The captured brigantine under the command of the quartermaster sailed south through the Providence Channel and set the captives off in boats near Hog Island where they could row ashore and secure passage back to the American colonies or Jamaica from Nassau. The prize ship then headed for Harbour Island with instructions to wait offshore until Captain Jack arrived.

The Avenger, now operating with a reduced crew, sailed north, back into the Florida Straits in hopes of one more plundering before meeting up with the quartermaster and the rest of the crew at Harbour Island. It was there that they would sell off the booty they had acquired on this trip.

Since the quartermaster was not aboard, Jack told Mary that in the event they did make a raid, she would be the one he would trust to tally their take and make sure that the men properly stored it in the hold. He announced to the crew that the cabin girl was to be the temporary quartermaster for the remainder of this voyage.

It wasn't long before she was to execute her new position. Less than a day later they came across a schooner leaving the colonies carrying indigo and silk to the West Indies. She pulled into the wind in surrender as soon as *The Avenger* was within gun range, and Jack promptly led most of the pirate crew aboard her. Mary, fully aware of the schooner's crew staring in disbelief that a woman would be serving as quartermaster on a pirate vessel, was filled with a strange sense of pride as she clambered, fully armed, aboard the captured ship to discharge her duties. Even though she held the purse strings while on *The Anne*, a ship from a world where money ruled, she could never had this level of authority or respect while aboard that vessel.

Down in the schooner's hold Mary examined the crates and counted the contents, writing it all down on a pad before instructing a waiting pirate to haul each one away. It was so businesslike and orderly, just like when she did the books on the plantation, and she felt quite comfortable and curiously at home in this new role.

When the hold had been emptied of cargo, Mary went up and joined Jack on deck. He was holding the schooner's captain at bay with his sword. "I have the tally, captain," she said in the most commanding voice she was able to muster.

"Please read it aloud, quartermaster," Jack answered without taking his eyes from his captive, watching the expression on his face as Mary read off the contents of the ship's hold.

"Are we missing anything, captain?" he asked when Mary had finished reading the list. Perhaps this was a rhetorical question, Jack had never received an affirmative answer to it, but it was one he always asked. "No? Then we shall bid you adieu."

Having been transferring the cargo, most of the crew was already back when Mary returned aboard *The Avenger*, and they greeted her with a multitude of accolades, including a hearty, "Good job," from the bosun when she turned her cutlass and pistol back in to him. Once *The Avenger* was under weigh again and the whole company was assembled on the deck for the customary celebration, it occurred to her just how well she had become integrated into the crew.

"You do realize, don't you, Mary," Jack told her while sporting a wide grin, "That since you actively participated in plundering today you are now officially a pirate like the rest of us." He handed her a beaker of rum. "A damned good one too. You looked magnificent wearing a sword."

"Should I wear one to bed tonight?" she teased, quietly so only he could hear, and then knocked back a swig of rum to conceal her smirk.

"Suits me," Jack raised his mug to her, "Provided that's all you'll be wearing." He turned around to lean against the rail, wrapping his arm around Mary as she snuggled up and rested her head on his right shoulder. They silently watched the sun set over a cloudless horizon and then headed to the captain's cabin that they now shared.

"I have a question for you, Jack," Mary asked as they cuddled in bed the next morning. "Why did you stay here in the Bahamas instead of turning privateer and going after the Spanish and the French? Surely the gold their ships carry is much better plunder than dry goods and sundry."

"That may be true, but we like to steer clear of politics. Besides, we make a living at what we do."

"But wouldn't more be better?"

Jack rolled onto his right side and rested on his elbow. "It's like this, Mary. No matter how much a pirate makes, he's going to spend it all as soon as he gets ashore. So if these lads can get whatever they want or need on what we make now without anyone getting hurt, why would I want to subject them to the chance of getting killed tangling with a warship for no further net benefit?"

"Doesn't anybody save for a rainy day?" Mary was shocked; this attitude was so carefree and unbusinesslike.

"Why? There are no rainy days in the Bahamas. We spend a month or so at sea, and then we enjoy life on shore until the money runs out and it's time to go back to sea again."

"So you never think of retiring, perhaps doing something else one day?" Mary's words were hopeful. She missed the luxuries of plantation life, and it was clear that Jack also enjoyed the finer things in life, but he was not picking up on her tone at all. What was she thinking, though? That he would somehow give up his pirate life and join her in her world? But, after the time she had spent with Jack, she wasn't even sure that was a world she was going to be comfortable in going back to anyhow, but if Jack were somehow to be in it with her..."

"Why on earth would we ever do that?" Jack interrupted her rambling train of thought and jumped out of bed. "We already have the perfect life. Come on, Mary; it's breakfast time."

After two more days of sailing, *The Avenger* rendezvoused with the brigantine five miles east of Harbour Island, and the two ships sailed together into port and anchored side by side. The quartermaster immediately transferred aboard *The Avenger* to give Jack his report.

"She leaks like a sieve, captain." The quartermaster said. "It's the worst case of shipworm I've ever seen. I had to have a crew at the pumps for the whole way over."

"Get the cargo ashore and take everything we can use from her then," Jack told him. "And we'll turn her over to the wreckers. We need to get *The Avenger* unloaded too." He nodded proudly towards Mary as he handed the quartermaster a ledger. "The cabin girl here did a first class tally on the contents of a schooner we hit on the way over."

Once all the barrels and crates were off the ships and on the dock, Jack, Mary, and the quartermaster met with the merchants to settle on prices. The pirates kept all of the rum and some of the flour and sugar they had seized, but the remainder of the plunder was sold. The crew was called to assemble on *The Avenger's* deck and the quartermaster announced the proceeds and distributed the shares. Captain Jack then proclaimed a furlough ashore, and the men excitedly disappeared heading, no doubt, for the establishments providing drink and entertainment in order to convert some of their cash into pleasure.

Jack instructed Mary to put her dress on, and after dressing himself in a fine tailored suit of black pants, purple silk shirt, and a burgundy brocade waistcoat, escorted her into the town proper.

Harbour Island was a unique place indeed. It was a bustling trading town filed with merchants with a longstanding tradition of having no problem with fencing pirate plunder. In fact, they welcomed the pirates. The merchandise they brought in was very much in demand throughout the colonies, and being able to purchase it at significantly lower than market price earned the traders a tidy profit. The good folks of Harbour Island were very wealthy and lived in opulent surroundings as a result of their relationship with the pirates of the Bahamas.

Jack took Mary to the house of Richard Thompson, one of Harbour Island's leading merchant-smugglers and a "good friend of the family" having also dealt with Jack's father in years past. They were treated by their host as if they were royalty, and after a sumptuous meal, were provided overnight accommodation in the Thompson's magnificent home, a house which would have rivaled any residence in the Carolinas.

Jack held the bedroom door open and watched Mary's face go from appreciative smile when she saw the four poster bed to open mouthed delight when she turned and laid her eyes on the claw footed bathtub full of water on the other side of the immense room. She rushed to it and plunged her hand in. "Perfect," she sighed, slowly swishing her fingers through the deliciously hot water. It smelled like the flowers in the garden outside. "It has been so long since I soaked in a bath."

Jack began to unfasten her dress while she was leaned over. "Then you shall wait no longer," he said. "And I shall bathe you."

Mary stood up and remained still while Jack peeled her dress and underclothing away...she was strangely comfortable being naked for him...then held her hand to ease her into the tub. He stripped to the waist and knelt next to the bath, then picked up a sponge, immersed it into the water, and poured some scented liquid from a purple glass bottle onto it. Mary watched as he worked the sponge between his hands until it became a mass of fragrant bubbles and moaned in delight when he proceeded to massage her shoulders with it. She closed her eyes as the sponge moved to her neck, and when she leaned forward, her back. Jack moved to a spot on the floor directly behind her and eased her back in the tub, then washed and caressed her breasts with the fragrant sponge. Mary craned her neck for Jack's wordlessly promised kiss and whispered, "Come in with me," to him as their lips drew together.

Jack released the sponge to float freely in the water, and after the kiss, stood up and unfastened his breeches in front of Mary's Mona Lisa smile to reveal a healthy shaft protruding from a curly sporran before her. Without thought she scooped up the sponge and squeezed it against the dark unkempt mass between his hips, then slid a soapy trail along the full length of his penis. She turned around, and now keeling in the tub, continued to soap up Jack's entire pubic area. Retracting his foreskin with her left hand while her right washed the glistening purple bulb with the sponge, she found herself disconnected from her surroundings, and her mind began to wander with the realization of what Jack might want her to do. While by no means worldly herself, Mary was nevertheless well aware of some of the scandalous activities that men would engage in with their slaves. They were things that could never be spoken about in mixed company, yet detailing them had served as a source of both disgust and giggles between Mary and her sisters. Since these acts were far beneath the dignity of a proper lady, perhaps this was one of the reasons that married women turned a blind eye to their husband's dalliances with slaves. Her sisters would certainly have called it degrading and humiliating, but to Mary it represented something else entirely; a means to give Jack pleasure. Hadn't he already released her from that world of artificial convention by telling her, in what seemed a lifetime ago, that her dignity was entirely up to her? Besides, she wanted this.

Still holding onto Jack's cock with her left hand, she plunged the sponge deep into the water with her right, squeezed the remaining soap out of it, and then used it to rinse him with the fresh water. Eyes looking up into his, the sponge fell from her hand as she leaned forward and opened her mouth. As Jack's cock slid across her tongue she closed her lips around it, and spurred on by his smile of approval, sucked it halfway in. His moan of delight was all the encouragement she needed to prompt her to rock her head back and forth, his member growing and beginning to tremble as it slid in and out. Jack entwined his fingers into Mary's hair, and she willingly submitted to his control of both depth and frequency until he suddenly gasped and held her head rigid while flooding her mouth with hot liquid. She instinctively swallowed and continued sucking while Jack eased his grip, until he leaned forward and kissed the top of her head. His whispered "Good girl," filled her with such warmth that it surely equaled the pleasure that she had just provided him.

Jack slid into the tub behind her, and Mary leaned against him in the still warm water, delighting in how his hands were exploring and fondling the front of her body while his lips and tongue caressed the right side of her neck. His left hand cradled her left breast while the fingers of his right teased the inside of her quivering thigh. The tub prevented her from spreading her legs any wider than they were, but that sense of confinement somehow added to the excitement, even more so when Jack's fingers began to toy with her clitoris. Mary's rapid breathing gave way to guttural moans when his thumb and forefinger closed around her engorged nipple and the gentle touches between her legs turned to rapid vibrations. Cocooned like this in Jack's embrace, it was only a matter of minutes before she threw her head back as he brought her to a wildly audible orgasm.

The next morning Jack took Mary to Harbour Island's marketplace. *The Avenger* wouldn't be leaving until high tide later in the afternoon, so they had ample time to stroll amongst the stalls and select delicacies from a wide variety of fruits and sweets to take back to their cabin for enjoying while they were back at sea. Within an hour, Mary was carrying as much as she was able in her arms. Jack purchased a straw basket for her, and then nodded towards a stand displaying brightly an assortment of brightly colored cotton clothing. "You need to be wearing something more comfortable while you're in the islands," he told her. "I'm going to buy you a new dress."

Jack selected a floral dress, and the proprietor showed Mary to a small room where she could try it on. The material felt so flimsy that it reminded Mary of the simple clothes that the slaves wore, but the vibrant colors were not at all the dull browns of slave attire. Neither was this dress the conservative clothing of a respectable South Carolina woman. The hem barely reaching her knees made her feel quite self-conscious when she emerged for Jack's review, but his approval overrode her qualms, and she happily continued the rest of the shopping trip looking, and no doubt feeling, like one of the island girls, latched onto Jack's right arm while he carried her bulky lady dress over his left. Her new dress was, of course, not for wearing aboard ship; but Mary was thrilled when Jack told her that it would be all right for her to do so in the privacy of their cabin.

6. Gold Rock

It was late morning on the second day after *The Avenger* left Harbour Island when Jack pointed towards a row of whitecaps in the sea directly ahead of them. "Do you see that, Mary?" he asked.

"Isn't that indicating there are reefs over there?"

"Indeed there are. We're heading into the most treacherous waters of the Bahamas; this upcoming reef has been an area of utter dread to most sailors ever since the Spanish explorer, Ponce De Leon, first discovered it."

"So why are we sailing so close to it then?" Mary was clearly anxious.

"Because," Jack grinned. "We are not most sailors." He picked up his spyglass and focused on the reefs. "Besides, home is just the other side of them; Gran Baha Island. You can't see it yet because the highest point is only sixty feet of elevation." He nodded, then turned back to Mary and stroked a flop of loose hair away from her face. "There is no need for you to worry," he said. "Go and fetch the shipmaster."

Mary was back in a matter of minutes, and as she and the shipmaster stepped up onto the foredeck, Jack relinquished control of the ship over to him. "Ship's master now has command," he called out for the entire ship's company to hear in his booming captain voice and then stepped aside to the rail.

"Thank you, captain," the shipmaster acknowledged Jack and then immediately called out an order, "Bosun, I need your men in the rigging," as he raised his spyglass to study the approaching reefs. He then consulted a chart he had brought with him, looked up again and barked out, "Helm, five degrees to port. Bosun, slow us down if you please."

The bosun was standing amidships as he called out various instructions to the individual crewmen who were handling the sheets and braces on deck or crawling around in the rigging above. Mary, quite visibly nervous as she stared at the white foam churning on the rapidly approaching reefs, stood close to a very calm Jack at the bow. He had previously explained to her how everyone on board was in their particular position because they were the best person for that job, and it was clear that he had utter confidence and trust in his crew. Unlike with the navy or merchant mariners, nobody could become an officer on a pirate vessel due to birthright or politics, and no amount of money could buy a pirate commission. As she listened to the shipmaster confidently calling out a series of small course corrections, Mary was very glad of that fact.

"See that cay ahead?" Jack nodded towards what looked like a small island or, more precisely, a big rock, peeking above the sea beyond the reef. "That's just off our home coastline, and that's where we're going. It is called Gold Rock."

The ship was almost at the reef, and Mary could now hear the breakers crashing across the shallow coral. Hitting a reef could rip the bottom from a boat and sink it within minutes. She tightly gripped the rail with her eyes fixed on the churning surf ahead when a clear area about fifty feet wide suddenly appeared right in the middle of the reef. *The Avenger* simply sped through it.

"Very nice shipmaster, good job," Jack called out calmly, his eyes still ahead. "Take us in and position the ship for careening."

"Aye, captain" the shipmaster replied casually, "Bosun, measurers to the bow if you will."

Two men rushed forward, one on each side of the bow, and began calling out depths as the ship sailed along the side of the huge rock that Jack had previously pointed out and into a huge bay fringed by a golden sand beach at least a mile wide behind it.

"And that, Mary," Jack said, standing behind and hugging her with his hands around her middle, "Is what makes our little home port so secure. Even if another ship were to stumble across that cut, it can only be crossed safely at high tide."

Now that *The Avenger* had cleared the reefs, the brilliant blue sea was calm and perfectly clear. Mary was amazed how she could see all the way to the bottom even though the water must have been at least forty feet deep. She scanned the shore to look for the pirate settlement, but there were no buildings or quays to be seen, just sand and trees. "Is this really your home port?" she asked Jack.

"Aye, it is."

"But I don't see anything."

"Look carefully," Jack told her. Sure enough, there was movement on the beach. There were people there, yes, but she still didn't see any structures.

"Of course not," Jack chuckled at her confusion. "It wouldn't be much of a secret hideout if we built it right out in the open, would it?"

"Furl the sails," the bosun shouted up to the men in the rigging as *The Avenger* made a turn parallel to the shore which depowered the sails and caused them to luff and flap in the warm breeze. "Drop the starboard anchor."

As the anchor splashed into the water the quartermaster ordered the crew to hang cargo nets over the sides of the ship while a dozen small boats started to row out from the shore towards them. Since the pirate base had no dock, the cargo was going to be loaded into boats to be taken ashore, but Jack explained that was something they had become most proficient at doing, and the ship would be completely unloaded by that evening. "And since we'll be getting off the ship too," he added, "you'd better go down to the cabin and change into your island dress."

Jack and Mary went ashore in one of the small boats midway through the unloading. By this time the beach was lined with stacks of barrels and crates, but the mood was more festive than work as the pirate crew took the time to reunite with their families, giving toys to the children, and their purses to their wives while sharing unabashed displays of affection with them. The work would get done, but as Mary was continuing to learn, these men always lived life in the present tense.

"A good haul, I hear, Jack." An authoritative female voice sounded over the crowd and Mary looked up to see a spritely, slender woman approaching them from the mangroves. She must have been sixty or more years old, her long grey hair was blowing behind her rugged tan face, but she had the gait of a twenty-year-old. She was wearing a loose fitting purple silk blouse tucked into a black skirt which reached to mid-calf in length, just above a pair of the finest quality black leather boots. "And this must be your hostage," she briefly wagged the mouthpiece of her clay pipe in Mary's direction without looking at her and walked directly up to Jack. "But I heard tell that you couldn't keep your mitts off her." She continued accusingly, standing just inches in front of him. Jack threw his arms around her, instantly melting her feigned stern demeanor, and they both erupted into laughter.

Jack pulled away, one arm still around the woman, and beckoned Mary towards them. "Mary Burleigh, I'd like you to meet my mother, Mary Read."

Mary approached the two of them cautiously, "My pleasure, ma'am," she said politely.

"I must say, you certainly don't look like a frumpy Carolina lady." The old woman's tone was warm and reassuring. "Where did you get such a delightful dress?"

"Jack bought it for me," Mary blurted out proudly.

"Did he now?" Jack's mother nodded vigorously and turned to Jack while flashing a quick grin. "Hmm," then hooked the fingers of her right hand under Mary's left. "I think you'd better come with me, and we ladies can have a nice quiet cup of tea while Jack and the men go about their work."

Mary was led along an elevated wooden walkway through the mangrove swamp beyond the beach and was fascinated by the abundance of wildlife everywhere she looked. Stone crabs scuttled amongst the mangrove roots, lizards with coiled tails ran along the walkway in front of them, small fish splashed in the water to escape the egrets, and the deep green canopy overhead was filled with the calls and squawking of a remarkable variety of birds. After a short walk they entered a clearing where there were wooden buildings on each side of the walkway. "These are all storage buildings," Jack's mother explained and then nodded to a cluster of smaller buildings further ahead. "And that's where the houses are." She pointed to the largest building to the left of them, "Over there is what we call our town hall," she said. "That's where we have all of our meetings, and it's also a general socializing area." She walked up to one of the small houses and opened the front door. "Come on in, Mary, this is my place. Let me show you around."

The house had two rooms. The one they were in had a bed to one side and a dining table and four chairs on the other, and to the back were two armchairs with a small table between them facing a large window which overlooked a garden. Mary was impressed with the quality of the furniture; much of it ornately carved mahogany and cherry wood cabinetry, and the curtains were made of heavy brocade.

The other room was a small but well-appointed kitchen with a kettle of hot water on the stove, which Jack's mother poured into a china teapot. "Go and have a seat on one of those armchairs," she said. "I'll be right in with the tea."

It wasn't until Mary was sitting down, talking to and enjoying tea and cake with this delightful Englishwoman, that it finally dawned on her who her hostess really was. "You're Mary Read, the pirate, aren't you?"

"One and the same, my girl." It was a proud response.

"I grew up hearing stories about you, Mrs. Read, but according to those stories you supposedly died almost thirty years ago in Jamaica."

"That's the thing with stories, isn't it? It's hard to know which ones are true."

"How did you come to be living on this island?"

The old lady poured second cups of tea. "We'd been captured and thrown in jail in Jamaica back then. Jack's father had been executed, hanged he was, and I was taken ill with fever and was ready to die, too, but then I remembered how Jack's father had sacrificed himself so his unborn child could live. Through the delirium it was like he was there reminding me of what he did, and in that same dream he told me it was my duty to pull through so he hadn't died in vain. The next day the fever broke and I was fine. Some friends paid off the guards to say I'd passed away that night, and I went with them to Cuba right after Jack was born." She looked up; her eyes were moist but bright. "I named him after his father, you know."

"And he is so proud to be the son of Jack Rackham."

Mary Read took a deep breath. "I was beside myself with rage with Calico Jack when he called for quarter. His whole life he'd been a scrapper, and this wasn't the first time we'd been in close quarters with the British Navy. Every time 'til then we'd fought like there was no tomorrow; if it meant death, then death by the sword was preferred by far. We'd always won out and been able to keep going, but his judgment got all cloudy like that day." Her tear filled eyes gazed out the window at some far off part of the sky.

Mary reached her right hand out to touch the top of the older woman's left, encouraging her to continue her story.

"Anyhow," Mary Read said, quickly recovering her composure and smiling at her guest. "I earned our keep serving drinks at one of the main taverns in town and managed to put bits aside, so when Jack was about seven years old I had enough to book passage for us to Nassau. When we arrived there, I set about to look up some of the old gang. I brought Jack up so as to keep his father's tradition alive, but I needed a ship to teach him what he needed to know about pirating, and we also needed a base to operate from. Fortunately, one of the old crewmembers I found in town was a Lucayan Indian that Jack's father had freed from the Spanish. He told us about this island. There used to be an Indian village here, back before they were all taken as slaves and worked to death on the Spanish Main. So," she finished her tea with a flourish, "A small group of us commandeered a sloop and here we are."

The women returned to the beach at dusk to find it transformed. Instead of stacks of crates a large bonfire had been constructed and was just being lit, and there were smaller cooking fires on which lobsters were being roasted and fish were being fried in vats of bubbling lard. A table was laid out with slices of mango, papaya and pineapple, and a man stood next to it flourishing a machete, hacking open coconuts and handing them out so people could drink the liquid out of them.

"There you are," Jack called out as he strolled up the beach to greet them. "And what tall tales has my mother been telling you?" he asked jokingly while putting his arm around Mary's shoulders.

Mary beamed at him. "Your mother is a remarkable lady."

"She is that." Jack nodded. "Our entire enterprise and everything you see around here is all due to her."

Jack seated Mary at the side of the beach then walked over to the tables and returned with a fried fish and a mound of rice on a plate in one hand and a freshly cooked lobster wrapped in seaweed in the other. They gobbled the feast using just their fingers, and after rinsing their hands off in a barrel of fresh water, filled the plate again with fruit and cuddled up together with it next to the dying fire. It was a clear night, and the constellations were particularly bright in the moonless sky. After the food was gone, they just lay there, his arm holding her against him, listening to the sea gently lapping at the shore until Jack told her that it was time to go to bed.

Jack's house was similar in layout to his mother's, but the furniture reminded Mary of his cabin on *The Avenger*. The bed, however, was larger and had velvet curtains tied back with gold cord to foot thick bedposts at each corner. Mary stood coyly next to the post at the foot of the bed, leaning against it with her hands behind her back and smiled. "How tired are you, Jack," she cooed.

"Never that tired," was the instant response. Jack slid his hands up her legs and had her dress up, and when she raised her arms, over her head and off in a single movement. She pulled his shirt off and nuzzled into his bare chest while he unbuckled his belt and dropped his breeches, then took her wrists in his left hand and held them against the post above her head and attacked her mouth with a ravenous kiss. Mary raised her left leg and rubbed her inside thigh against him while his free hand squeezed and massaged her smooth bottom. They slowly parted from the kiss, and Jack moved her a couple of feet to his left, sat her up on the foot of the bed and stood between her spread legs. As he pulled her against him for a kiss she clung tightly to his shoulders and rocked back and forth, desperately trying to impale herself on Jack's rigid rod. "You want it, don't you?" He teased, but before she could reply he pushed her back onto the bed, put his hands behind her knees and spread her wide before ramming his cock into her. It took only three thrusts before she screamed in delight. He withdrew and slid her now limpid body up onto the bed, then lay down next to her. He once again pinned her wrists over her head and turned her sideways so she had her back to him and reached across her sweating body to tease her nipples. The restraint and stimulation soon had Mary panting again, and feeling Jack's still stiff cock behind her, she started to rock her hips back and forth. Mary expected to be penetrated again, but when she realized where Jack intended to do it, she began to panic and fruitlessly tried to struggle away. This was something that men only did to slaves, why was he going to do it to her? She was panting hard and violently shaking her head from side to side. Did Jack see her as a slave? She exhaled loudly and with the realization that was obviously not the case, Jack was the consummate anti-slaver. She rammed her face into the sheet. Except for when he was taking her sexually he treated her as an equal, and his general attitude towards her clearly conveyed his genuine caring. In matters of sex, however, he always dominated her. This act was simply another expression of Jack's incredible passion.

She released herself to the moment, became compliant and willingly gave her body over to Jack's desire. "That's right, Mary. Just relax," He whispered as he effortlessly rolled her over until she was face down, and positioned himself between her forcefully parted legs. His moisture covered penis slid easily into her bum, but he moved slowly until she had become sufficiently receptive, then slid his right hand under her and roughly worked her clitoris with his fingertips while pumping back and forth with his hips. Mary's initial shock was soon inflamed to wild passion as she writhed, pinned beneath Jack's body, until the both of them trembled and then froze in unison while Jack pulsed and ejected deep inside her.

After a long minute, he slowly slid off to her right side, rolled her over and cocooned her in his arms with her head nuzzled against his chest while he drifted into glorious slumber. Mary wrestled against the impending twilight of sleep in order to fantasize about how the two of them might somehow remain together. Even if Jack were willing to live in civilized society with her, she could never ask him to give up this life he so clearly loved. The islands and his passions were intertwined, perhaps they were even interdependent. Would he even be the same Jack without them? She also began to question whether, even after this brief time, if she could ever again be happy in a place where the opulence of life was dependent upon the toil of indentured human beings. Her eyes fluttered closed. All she knew was the contentedness she felt at that moment.

7. Quandary

The following afternoon Jack was summoned to a private meeting with his mother. While he might have been the captain of the pirate ship, Mary Read was the island matriarch, and she was going to have a sit down, serious talk with her son.

"So tell me, Jack, just what are you planning to do with Mary?" Jack's mother put the question he had been avoiding to him point blank; that was her way.

"I don't rightly know, mother." Jack sank into a chair. "The truth is, things just got carried away, and I never stopped to think it through."

"Richard, your quartermaster, tells me you had eyes for her from day one. What was it about her?"

"I can't even rightfully answer that either, but he is right. I was drawn to her right off the bat. It was almost like she bewitched me."

"Nonsense, what hooked you is the fact that she stood up to you. I always said that the only type of woman you'd fall for was one who wouldn't cow down to you."

"Like my mother, eh?" Jack chucked. It was true, Mary by name, Mary by nature. They really did have a lot in common.

"Ah, you really are your father's son, Jack," she added proudly. "Believe me, I do understand. But the fact is that how you got here just begs the question, doesn't it? And keep in mind that it is your own bloody fault that you're in this mess."

Jack looked up, took in a deep breath and exhaled slowly through his mouth. "I suppose when you look at the facts, it is really pretty simple." Jack nodded slowly as he spoke. "We took her as a hostage and offered a business deal to her family for her return, so we have to honor it. Even more important, the crew is entitled to their ransom money. My duty dictates by my action." He forced a smile. "So I really don't have a choice, do I?"

"Oh Jack." The old woman slowly shook her head. "Mary's a lovely woman, and it's pretty clear that she's become mightily attached to you." Her expression became a wide-eyed glare. "Now, I didn't raise my son to be a callous brute, did I?"

There was silence for almost a minute before her face softened. She reached over and firmly took Jack's hands up in hers. "Think it through, Jack," she said, shaking them. "Even if you do decide to go ahead and break her heart, what's that going to do to you? How are you going to end up feeling if you let her go?"

Jack wasn't able to formulate his next question, but his mother answered it anyway. "You'll figure it out, Jack," she told him with a knowing smile. "Something always comes up when you set your mind to it."

The following weeks were idyllic. Jack and Mary explored the forests in the center of the island, and he showed her the caves that the Lucayan Indians once used for their ceremonies. The two of them swam and played together, blissfully naked in the freshwater pools. Evening meals three times a week were enjoyed communally with the rest of the crew on the beach, Willum had become extremely popular with his ability to not only capture wild pigs but prepare them with rubs and roast them to perfection over a smoky wood fire, but the rest of the time Jack and Mary just enjoyed each other's company. Nights continued to be eminently satisfying, sex for them was never routine, and Mary came to the strange realization that, while she enjoyed his gentle sensuality, she derived the most pleasure when Jack was aggressive with her, when he simply took her as if he were giving in to his primal drives. Mary was freely experiencing the passion she had always dreamed of, the abandonment of thinking and simply giving herself over to the moment. Yet, even at his most aggressive, Jack was always in control, and it was clear that her pleasure was more important to him than his own, and because of that she trusted him. She confided to Jack that she loved it when he held her down to have his way, any way, with her, and it was after that admission that a new phase of their nocturnal life emerged.

That following evening when Mary was lying naked on top of the bed waiting for Jack to join her, he knelt next to her instead of lying down, and smiling at her, untied the cord from the bed curtain and wrapped it around her right wrist. She compliantly watched him bind her wrists together. He took the other end and tied it to the top of the bed, then slid off it, went to the foot and pulled her legs until the cord was taught and her arms were stretched above her head. Quickly untying the cords from around the posts at the bottom of the bed and affixing them to her ankles, he positioned her with her legs spread wide; each of her ankles firmly attached to a bed post, and then crawled onto the bed between them. He nuzzled against the inside of her thighs, and Mary pulled against the restraints, but she was firmly bound and unable to break free of them. He teasingly began kissing between her legs until she began to writhe against the restraints and then started to arouse her with the tip of his tongue. The fact she could pull against the cords but was unable to break free of them, enhanced her excitement as he proceeded to worked her to a gasping frenzy with his tongue. He took her right to her edge, one moment more and satisfaction would have been hers, but he knowingly moved away from that spot and instead continued to kiss and lick up her torso, across her breasts and up the side of her neck where he held her head steady and forced his tongue into her mouth. She had never tasted herself before. She hungrily participated in this fevered kiss, spurred on by Jack's index finger which was now dancing on her clitoris, but as soon as her hips began to buck against it, he stopped and pulled away, clearly excited by her gasping, pleading mouth. He returned to the foot of the bed and untied her ankles, put one on each of his shoulders and moved his body on top of hers forcing her legs up and apart while pushing his cock deep inside her, then clamped his mouth down on hers again controlling her breathing while he pounded into her. Mary had never experienced the intensity of multiple orgasms before. Jack would most certainly have to tie her up again.

Consciously or not, Jack had pushed his earlier conversation with his mother into the recesses of his mind and had simply been enjoying each day at a time since then. December came, however, and it was the quartermaster who brought up the inevitable. He caught up with Jack when he was alone in the town hall.

"It's time, Captain," the Quartermaster began, "And it's my obligation on behalf of the crew to remind you we'd better plan to set sail and collect the ransom on Miss Mary." The quartermaster looked at the floor, stroked his chin and muttered, "It's a damn shame that she hadn't elected to join the crew that day and instead became a hostage, eh?"

"How long do we have?" Jack was solemn, his voice a monotone.

"We should push off tomorrow, the day after tomorrow at the latest." The quartermaster looked up to study Jack's sullen face and shook his head. "Jack, Jack," he repeated while grabbing a bottle of rum and pouring out a full beaker. "I can see I'm going to have to console you with some reality talk, the way I have for many a lovesick pirate over the years. Now, you drink this down and let's us revisit how all of this came to be."

He poured a second drink for himself and joined Jack with a hearty swig. "First off," he said, "you paid for her. Do you really think you'd have had a lady of breeding coming into your bed if she'd perceived that she might have had a choice in the matter? Now, don't get me wrong.

All the crew, me included, have really come to like Miss Mary, but the reality is that she's just been sucking up to you to protect her until she could get safely home. Getting you to feel all mushy and emotional over her was just part of her strategy to ensure that she would have the captain looking after her." He finished his rum. "You really can't blame her, you know. In fact there's no fault anywhere. You just need to accept that you've had a time with her, but now it's time for all concerned to move on."

Jack studied the contents of his mug. The quartermaster was right; this had all started with him paying for Mary to keep her out of the hands of the others. It seemed like such a noble gesture then, he hadn't realized at the time he was really doing it because he wanted her for himself. He was in the same boat as any other pirate would be in the same situation, and he should be content to have enjoyed the time he'd had her. What lady takes up voluntarily with pirates?

By the time the rum was finished Jack was nodding in agreement, and he finally slapped his hand on the quartermaster's shoulder. "Thanks, Richard," he laughed. "I bloody well needed that."

"We're all right here then, Jack?"

"Damn right I am," Jack roared up at the ceiling. "Get the Avenger ready to sail, and let's get her the hell out of here."

Jack kept away from Mary as much as he could for the next day by busying himself with readying the ship. Had she really played him? Had all this supposed affection towards him simply been an elaborate ruse on her part to ensure her safety until she could be free of the pirates and go back home where she belonged? He'd be her private laughing stock if all that were true.

He decided it would be best that when the Avenger went back to sea, he would have Mary treated as a guest, properly the hostage that she was, back on her way to being ransomed. She would be put in her own cabin, wear the dress that she came in, and he would not require cabin girl or any other duty of her. It had to be over.

Mary could easily read that Jack was in turmoil, and she desperately wanted to help, but rationalized that he was the one in control of the situation and there was nothing she would be able to do. If only he would ask her, she would happily stay with him on this island, but suggesting it to him would be unfair and put him in conflict with what she knew was his responsibility to his crew. She wouldn't do that to him. Neither could she ask him to come and join her in her world; a world representing everything he was fighting against. Still, if Jack really felt about her the way his actions suggested, the way he had treated her since they met, then how could he willing to just let her go like this? Even more disturbing was that they had not even discussed this. Had she really just been his plaything these past weeks and nothing more? Had he made her feel secure simply to relax her into being a willing partner for his sexual proclivities? Being forced apart from Jack was going to rip her apart emotionally, and she knew she would never recover from it, but no-one was ever going to know that. Mary determined from that point on to present herself to the world with steeled reserve.

The Avenger set sail on time, and a few days into the journey, Jack, who had been avoiding Mary all this time, went up to her where she was standing by the rail to tell her that they were soon scheduled to meet up with *The Anne*. He had known what he needed to do from the day he discussed it with his mother but had never been able to summon the courage to act on it. Now, with only hours before Mary would be gone forever, this was his last chance to put his plan in place. He grabbed her and gazed longingly into her eyes, and at that moment didn't care if he ended up humiliating himself in front of her or not. He had to confront her. "I love you, Mary," he said and then pulled her tightly towards him, his face over her shoulder so he didn't have to see if she was laughing at him. Those words, in a nutshell, summarized his entire plan. How would she respond?

Two hours later the lookout called, "Sails ahoy," and Jack ordered *The Avenger* to heave to and lower a boat. The quartermaster and two crewmen escorted Mary into the dinghy, there were no goodbyes, and Mary stared back at *The Avenger* for as long as she was able to pick Jack out on deck while the crewmen silently rowed her over to *The Anne*.

8. Reunion

The pirates in the rowboat secured bow and stern lines to the hull of *The Anne* and the quartermaster clambered up the rope ladder that had been dropped over the side to them. "Good afternoon, Captain Fordham," he bellowed, as he hoisted himself aboard and casually rested his right hand on the handle of one of the pistols in his belt. "I trust you have our money?"

"I do indeed, sir. And do I have your assurance than Miss Burleigh is unharmed?"

"I can assure you that she has been treated well, and not one member of the ship's crew has as much as laid a finger on a hair of her head." His teeth flashed as he delivered his flamboyant response.

"Very well, here is your ransom." He handed the quartermaster a small pouch. "In gold, as you demanded. It's all there."

The quartermaster bounced the bag in his right hand and had a quick look inside. "I'm sure it is, captain," he said casually. "And if it's not, we'll just blow you out of the water." He tied the pouch to his belt and backed up to the side of the ship. "Miss Burleigh is free to come aboard," he called to the men in the boat below.

Mary's head soon appeared, and the quartermaster extended his left arm to her and smiled. "You take care now, lass," he said, helping her on board, and then quickly debarked down the ladder.

Captain Fordham nodded and smiled at Mary, clearly relieved to have her back safely aboard; then immediately called out for *The Anne* to make sail. Mary intended to stand at the rail and watch the dinghy row away, but her mother suddenly appeared, pushing through the frenzy of sailors on deck and rushed up to greet and latch on to her daughter with an overly enthusiastic hug. "We were all so worried, Mary," she said, panting but with clear relief in her voice. "Are you really all right?"

"I'm fine, mother," Mary responded quizzically, "But, but what are you doing here?"

"Your father hasn't been well these past few months so I came in his stead. Actually, I would have insisted on coming anyway." With her hands on her daughter's shoulders, Anne first scanned her up and down then gingerly touched her hair. "Look at you Mary; your skin is so dark and your hair needs a good washing, and," she fussed, "we'd better get you out of this sun right away. Come with me." Anne grabbed Mary's hand and led her below deck and into the owner's cabin.

"I really am fine, mother," Mary protested.

"What do you mean, 'fine'?" Anne questioned her. "You've been away for almost three months, you were abducted during a pirate raid and held hostage for ransom. How could you possibly be fine?"

"I was treated well," Mary smirked and quickly changed the subject with, "but, look at you, my mother, at sea of all things."

"I was so worried about you, Mary; I just had to be here."

"Well since you are here," Mary sat on the bed and patted the blanket next to her. "Tell me about what's happening at home. How is everybody?"

"Other than your father feeling poorly, everything's pretty much the same. The slaves cleared two new rice fields, but they may have to sit fallow for the next season on account of those two planters you bought being stolen by the pirates who abducted you." Ann looked quizzically at her daughter. "I rather expected to find you a distraught mess, so I'm quite comforted to see you so remarkably calm. You weathered it well."

She pushed a lock of hair from her daughters face and tucked it behind her ear. "So, what were your thoughts while all of this was happening?"

"I had at first thought Captain Fordham to be a coward for not fighting when the pirates attacked us," Mary confessed. "But on reflection I now realize he acted correctly. He told me to be quiet and stay in my cabin, and if I hadn't been so curious about what was going on, I might not have even been discovered." Mary turned sideways and touched the back of her mother's right hand. "I want father to know that it really wasn't the captain's fault that I was captured."

"Merchant ship captains all know the drill." Anne said knowingly. "Attempting to fight against a pirate crew would be futile and result in far greater loss than just letting them take the cargo. Even so, Captain Fordham was so devastated that you were taken hostage that he gave his earnings from the trip towards paying your ransom. His only thought these past months has been getting you back."

"How could there have been earnings from that trip? The pirates took the entire cargo."

"As it turned out, the amount of ambergris Captain Fordham returned with still made it a profitable venture." Anne made a quick smile and again lurched forward and threw her arms around Mary again. "But the most important thing of all is that you're back with us."

"And as you can see, I'm all right." Mary gently pushed back and stood up; her mother's ebullience, something she had grown up with, was now uncomfortably smothering.

"And you're also incredibly lucky," Anne continued. "I've never heard of a woman who was able to keep her honor after being abducted by pirates." Anne studied her daughter's unsuccessful attempt to conceal a smirk. "Or was that brute lying?"

"Oh, he was telling the truth, about the crew that is. The captain saw to that."

"So he could have you for himself?" Anne's right hand covered her wide open mouth; her eyes became saucers, and her left hand gripped onto the edge of the bed.

Mary quickly sat beside her again and put her arm around her shoulders. "It wasn't like that at all, mother. Captain Read was so gallant, and he even gave me my own cabin. It was me who seduced him." She grasped her mother's hands and held them to her lap. "He's the most incredible man I've ever met."

"What! What are you telling me, Mary?"

"I'm telling you that the reason I'm aboard now is to let you and everyone else at home know that I am fine, and you can all stop worrying about me. I love him, mother, and I'm going back to him."

Anne's mouth opened wide, and she struggled to eke out a breathy, "Wha...wha...what?"

Mary stood up and pulled her dumbfounded mother to her feet next to her. "You'll see. We'd better get back up on deck, mother," she said, leading the way out of the cabin and up the stairs.

There was a strong northeasterly wind blowing, and *The Anne* was making good time, but Captain Fordham stood anxiously at the aft rail with his spyglass trained on *The Avenger* which was churning through the water off the Anne's starboard stern and gaining on them. "Damn it," he muttered. "What does that infernal Captain Read want now?"

"He is awaiting my signal," Mary announced loudly as she climbed the stairs up to the aft deck and stood next to him. "If I choose to stay, I am supposed to stand here and wave him off, but if I want to go back with him, then," she reached behind her neck to adjust the fastenings on her dress which quickly fell to the floor around her ankles, "I do this." Mary stepped out of the heavy garment, picked it up, and handed it to her speechless mother who, huffing and puffing had just caught up with her. The pretty island dress, the one that Jack had bought for her, fluttered in the breeze around Mary's thighs as she excitedly waved both her hands above her head. "Turn into the wind, captain," she said with a sudden authority, "And make ready for *The Avenger* to pull alongside." She turned and matched his defiant glare. "You had better do it now, Captain, or *The Avenger* will force you to stop by taking out your mast."

Captain Fordham pushed past the helmsman and barked instruction down to the crew to comply with Mary's order, then turned back to Anne. "It seems that your daughter's turned pirate on you," he said in disgust and descended the stairs.

"Are you sure about this, Mary?" Anne was suddenly calm and her voice seemed oddly understanding.

Mary beamed at her. "Oh, yes, yes, yes," she said nodding wildly. "Please give me your blessing."

"I can't possibly do that until I know that he'll be good for you?"

"He's perfect for me, mother, and he loves me."

Anne's smile was completely unexpected. She began to say something, but her mouth froze, and she suddenly became transfixed and her hands locked onto the rail like a bird's claws. She was staring at the flag flying from the approaching vessel. "I'm going over with you," she said abruptly, not taking her eyes from *The Avenger*. She took a deep breath to regain her composure before she was able to look back to her clearly confused daughter. "I have an insatiable need to meet this captain of yours." Anne said as she slowly loosened her grip on the rail. "Doesn't a mother have a right to know the man who was able to steal her daughter's heart?"

Mary went aboard *The Avenger* first and rushed into Jack's waiting arms to the wild cheers of the pirate crew while Anne was still being assisted onto the deck. "Tell me, captain," Anne bellowed towards the man who was lip locked with her daughter. "What gives you the right to fly the Skull and Cutlasses?" She glared while the captain and Mary slowly parted, but as soon a she saw his face she gasped an inaudible, "Jack?"

"My name is Captain Jack Read," Jack boomed out, his left arm clasped tightly around Mary. "My father was Captain Jack Rackham, and as his son I claim every right to fly our family flag. So now, my lady, just who might you be and what are you doing aboard my ship?"

"Jack," Mary quickly spoke up. "This is my mother, Anne Burleigh. She wanted to meet you." She reached out with her left hand. "Mother, this is Jack."

"At your service, Mrs. Burleigh," Jack removed his hat and bowed courteously while Mary slipped free of his arm and stood next to her mother. "Welcome aboard *The Avenger*," Jack continued. "I'm delighted to make your acquaintance."

"Thank you, captain," Anne replied, recapturing her ladylike demeanor.

"But tell me, how is it that a lady such as yourself is aware of pirate flags?" Jack asked.

"Oh, I know, I mean I have read a lot about pirates, captain. Mary might have told you that we have quite an extensive library at our home. I remember reading that a flag is a rather like a signature, something unique and belonging to a particular captain so only he can have it. In fact, I remember reading that Calico Jack's flag is the most famous of all. I know that he's dead, so I naturally wondered how his flag could still be in use."

"You might say that I'm continuing his family tradition," Jack replied proudly.

Mary was perplexed by this conversation; she had never known her mother to ever express either any interest in or knowledge about pirates, but she felt an uncomfortable need to be a part of the conversation. "Jack's mother is Mary Read, the famous woman pirate," she interjected.

"Mary Read is alive?" Anne's lower jaw dropped, but she quickly recovered. "I thought she had died around the same time as Calico Jack?"

"She is alive, mother. I have met her, and she is an absolutely delightful lady."

The quartermaster interrupted the conversation. "Excuse me, Captain, but I think we'd best be pushing off."

"Of course," Jack answered. "Mrs. Burleigh, you're welcome to stay on board with us as our honored guest if you'd like. You can spend some time with your daughter, and we'll drop you off in Nassau in a few weeks so you can return home from there. But if you want to return with Captain Fordham, you'd better get back aboard his ship now." He obviously intended this as a gracious way to tell Mary's mother to leave his ship.

Mary grasped her mother's arm to walk her to the rail and say goodbye, but Anne calmly patted her daughter's hand, looked squarely at Jack and said, "I appreciate your gracious offer, captain, and I would love to stay aboard. Thank you."

Jack, clearly surprised by Anne's acceptance, nodded a wry smile of approval towards the ladies. "Then Mary will show you to your cabin," he said.

Anne was to be bunked in Mary's old cabin. Mary took her below deck to show her where she would be staying, but immediately closed the door behind them as soon as they were inside. "What in the world are you thinking, mother? You've no business being aboard a pirate ship."

"You're my daughter and you're here, aren't you?"

"Of course I am." Mary was flabbergasted. "But this is my life now. Your life is on a," she sputtered, "On a plantation in South Carolina."

"You've only been out here a short time, Mary. So how is it that can you be so certain that this is the life you really want to lead?"

"Jack and I love each other and this is his world, so I want to be in it with him."

"It's the man you're in love with, Mary, not this life. You belong in the world I raised you in. Now, I'm not going to find fault with who you fall in love with, but I will tell you that there's many a pirate who made his money and went on to a respectable life as a gentleman ashore. So think it through, Mary. If he does indeed love you, consider that you could have both Jack and a proper life?"

"I've already thought about that," Mary responded thoughtfully. "But I don't think I could ever go back, even if Jack were to go with me." She sighed, and then abruptly added, "Which he won't."

"Don't be so hasty, Mary, why don't we just wait and see. True love can cause a man to do almost anything, you know."

The day had been eventful and full of unexpected turns, not the least of which being the appearance of her mother, but Mary was happily back aboard *The Avenger* with Jack. She closed the door to the captain's cabin that evening with a sense of contentment. It was now just the two of them again. Jack looked at her adoringly when she leaned her back against the door and smiled seductively at him, slowly dragging the fingers of her right hand up her thigh and pulling the hem of her dress up just above her right hip. "Cabin girl reporting for duty, sir," She whispered, panting with anticipation. "I am yours for whatever you desire?"

9. Capture

Anne woke early the next morning, and desperate for a cup of coffee, made her way to the galley where a peg legged man with his back to her was working over the stove. "Excuse me," she said, causing him to turn around. His face instantly burst into animation. "Well, blast me," he said, his eyes blinking, "If it ain't Anne Bo..."

"Burleigh," Anne excitedly drowned his voice out as she stepped close to him. She placed her right index finger across her lips. "It's Burleigh," she repeated in a normal voice as she dropped her finger to her side.

"Heh heh heh," Andy chuckled. "Whatever you say, Anne."

"It's good to see you again, Andy." Anne quickly looked down and back up again. "Sorry about your leg."

"No problem there; I'm alive, I got work, and I get daily rum," Andy replied, "And there ain't too many of the old crew still able to boast that." He picked up a ladle, filled a mug from a pot on the stove and handed it to Anne. "Here you go; you always liked coffee in the morning."

Anne eagerly quaffed back half of the bitter brew. "Thanks Andy. You could say I needed that."

"So, you're Miss Mary's mother, eh. " He chuckled again. "That sort of helps explain everything."

"What do you mean?"

"As you've might have noticed, Captain Jack's the spittin' image of his father in looks, and he's that way in action too. He's been immune to every woman he's ever come across 'til your daughter shows up, and, well, look at them together and you can see for yourself. He's head over heels, just like old Calico Jack was for you. It only makes sense that she's your bloodline."

"Listen, Andy. You've got to keep this quiet for me. All right?"

"My lips'll be mum on it, Anne, but it seems to me that you're going to have to come clean about it yourself before too long." He laughed again. "And that's gonna be coming as one hell of a shock for Miss Mary."

"I know," Anne sighed and took another slug of the hot drink. "But I have to think about it for a while longer because I'm not yet sure how to go about it."

Anne was amazed when she saw her daughter dressed in a shirt and breeches when they met up on deck later that morning. "So you actually are a member of this pirate crew, then?" She asked Mary.

"She is indeed," Jack said, walking up behind them. "Your daughter has served as well as any on board." He gave Mary quick hug with his left arm. "And I'm sorry to interrupt, Mrs. Burleigh, but right now I'm going to have to have her on duty."

"Why is that?" Anne queried. "Is there to be action?"

"Indeed there is. We are approaching a merchant vessel, and this ship needs to be getting about its business. Upper deck will be rather busy and probably no place for a lady for the next few hours Mrs. Burleigh, so may I suggest you wait in your cabin until our, um, transaction has been completed."

"If it's all the same to you, captain, I'd rather stay on deck and watch."

"I suppose," Jack looked thoughtful and spoke slowly.

"Jack, I don't think that's a good idea," Mary began, but Jack cut her off and pulled her aside. "It shouldn't be a problem," he whispered to her. "They're not likely to resist."

"I know," Mary whispered back. "But I don't think my mother understands."

"Of course, I know what is happening, Mary." Anne had walked up to them and was listening to their conversation. She pointed her chin towards Jack. "Captain, please, there is no need to patronize me."

"Very well, you are welcome to remain on deck." Jack grinned and nodded at her. "But do pay attention because if this ship we're approaching chooses to fight us I'll want you to get below right away. I can't have you getting hurt."

"That is reasonable captain, thank you."

Mary accompanied Jack to the bow and he raised his spyglass. "She's a good sized sloop," he said, "Must be close to a hundred tons," he lowered the glass, "Which also means she could be carrying as many as eight cannon. Mary, go and fetch the quartermaster."

Anne had followed them towards the bow so she could listen in on the conversation, and right hand holding onto the rigging for support as the boat rose and fell, she watched Mary scurrying nimbly across the ship on her errand. It was only a few minutes before she had returned with the quartermaster.

"What do you make of her, quartermaster?" Jack asked.

"That's a mighty fine looking ship, captain," the quartermaster said as he focused the spyglass ahead. "And she's surely seen us because she's tightened up her sails. That captain plans to run," he grinned.

"That's not going to do them much good," Jack replied.

"Aye, she's too heavily loaded. Still, if they are running then they're probably going to end up wanting to fight once we get close."

"Agreed," Jack said. "Our advantage is that we're both on a starboard tack and beating into the wind like this heels us over, so if we approach her wide from the port side her guns won't be able to reach us. Get your boarding party ready."

"Aye aye, captain."

Jack turned and shouted out to the crew. "We have a runner, lads, so let's show 'em our colors. Raise the Skull and Cutlasses. Bosun, distribute pistols and cutlasses all around. Jermy, play us a tune if you please."

The crew cheered as the flag was raised to the rousing melody of Jermy's flute, and they rapidly donned their weapons. After Mary had strapped her cutlass belt on and slipped a pistol into place, she quickly went to check on her mother before returning to Jack's side.

"This is all so exciting," Anne said, surprising Mary with what could only be described as a smile of approval. "Hurry now," she said, scooting her off, "Don't you worry about me."

"Why is all of this not shocking her?" Mary muttered to herself as she returned to the bow. How could a genteel lady calmly watch her daughter readying for battle?

Once she was next to Jack again, however, Mary's head was clear and she was completely focused on the task at hand.

The bow of *The Avenger* was almost level with the stern of the sloop, and Jack bellowed out for it to heave to, but there was no response and the merchant ship pulled even more into the wind in defiance. "Hold course and open the starboard gun ports," Jack shouted out. "Gunners, target the mast on my command. We'll take her on her lee."

The sloop tried to pull away into the wind, but the course change cost it speed, and while further away now, *The Avenger* was almost alongside her and she was in range. "Fire," Jack called out.

There were a series of deafening explosions, and the ship lurched to the left as all four guns fired. The sloop temporarily disappeared behind a wall of acrid smoke. All pirate hands ran to the starboard side, anxiously waiting for the smoke to clear and then cheered in unison.

The sloop was stopped, its mast was down, and her sails were tangled in the fallen rigging. "Tack around and prepare to board," Jack shouted out.

The Avenger turned, and the wind now astern, she calmly sailed up next to her stricken quarry. The pirates latched onto the hull with grappling hooks and swarmed aboard. There was no resistance, and the sloop's captain surrendered to *The Avenger's* quartermaster the instant he swung aboard and drew his cutlass.

Ten minutes later the quartermaster returned to the pirate ship. "Captain," he addressed Jack excitedly. "This was her maiden voyage; it's a brand new sloop, and her hold is full of rum. There's too much cargo for us to take it all aboard, but the ship itself is a real prize, too. We can get her jury rigged and ready to sail in less than a day; what say we do that and then take her home for proper repairs. We can set the captain and officers ashore along the way."

"An excellent plan, quartermaster; let's go aboard so I can meet this ship's captain."

It was only after Jack had left with the quartermaster that Mary realized that her mother had been standing close to them this entire time. "Mother," she admonished. "Didn't Jack tell you to go below if there was any action?"

"And leave my daughter up here on deck? I should have been worried sick. Besides, that was all really quite exhilarating." She turned to watch Jack and the quartermaster nimbly board the captured vessel. "I like your Jack, Mary; not only is he handsome, but he's also a man of action." Anne turned back and looked askance at her daughter. "Don't give me that look of disapproval, young lady. I'm your mother."

"But I've never even imagined you anything like this. You're completely out of character, mother. What happened to your 'always act like a lady' maxim that you beat into our heads growing up?"

"We're not in South Carolina at the moment, Mary, we're on a pirate ship. Surely that gives license to set certain otherwise requisite behaviors aside, don't you think?"

Anne continued to give her daughter pause that evening by joining the crew's on deck celebration, heartily swigging back rum from a tin mug and acting almost as if she were one of them. "Nicely done, captain," she tipsily raised her mug while calling out to Jack. "That was a fine capture today, indeed."

It took three days for the two ships to make it back to Gran Baha Island, but they did so without incident. The captured sloop, her broken mast lashed back together but now considerably shorter and flying only half of her sails, closely tailed *The Avenger* as they navigated the cut in the reef at high tide and was run towards the beach until she bottomed out on the sand. Lines were run out and staked so the ship would remain upright when the tide went out; in this way she would be both easy to unload and to check for damage. At a minimum, the sloop was going to need a new mast, but that would easily be accomplished on this island due to the abundance of sturdy and straight island pines.

The Avenger anchored in the bay, and Jack rowed Mary and her mother ashore in one of the ships boats. Anne was facing the island when suddenly her hands began to fidget uncontrollably as the figure of an older woman standing on the shore came into focus. "What's wrong, mother?" Mary asked.

"There are some things I need to tell you," Anne blurted out, simultaneously grabbing tightly onto her daughter's right hand. "Things you need to know."

The dinghy scraped bottom, and Jack jumped out to pull it up onto the shore, and then stood at the bow to assist the ladies out.

"We'll have plenty of time for you to tell me things while we're here, mother," Mary said as she stood up and took Jack's hand, then stepped out of the boat and hugged his mother. "Mrs. Read," she said. "I'd like you to meet my mother, Anne Burleigh."

Anne kept her head down as she stepped out of the boat, but once ashore and standing in front of the two women, she slowly raised it.

"Bloody hell," Mary Read shrieked, slapped her right hand over her wide open mouth then dropped it again. "It's Anne."

"Hello, Mary," Anne replied, her stoicism yielding to an uncontrollable smile. "It's good to see you again."

The women fell into an almost tearful embrace while Mary and Jack looked. "How, how is it that the two of you know one another?" Jack eked out in disbelief. Mary had no words at all.

"We'd better all go to my house and sit down," Jack's mother smiled and nodded at her son. "And I suspect that this is going to call for something a little stronger than a cup of tea."

The four of them walked briskly along the mangrove trail and into town without any further conversation, and once inside the house all Mary was able to verbally compose was a quizzically demanding, "Mother?" as she stared at Anne.

"She doesn't know does she?" Jack's mother's question was pointedly direct to Anne, who just slowly shook her head and seemed unable to look anyone in the eye. "Would you like me to tell her, Anne?" Mary Read prompted.

"Tell me what?" Mary's voice became loud with insistence. "Would one of you please let me know what is going on here?"

"Mary," Mary Read began. "Long ago, way back before you were born, your mother and I were friends. Good friends. We met in Nassau where you could say we both worked in the shipping industry together."

Mary's eyes bored into her mother. "Nassau? I thought you'd never been out of South Carolina?"

"It's all rather complicated, Mary," Anne admitted, diverting her eyes to her old friend.

"Are you going to tell her, Anne, or shall I?" Jack's mother calmly gave Anne the option. "Your daughter needs to know."

"I think you'd better continue," Anne said quietly.

All eyes converged back on Mary Read who silently picked up her pipe and looked directly at Mary Burleigh. "Your mother and I served alongside each other under Calico Jack Rackham, Mary." Mary Read spoke with pride. "Back then she went by the name of Anne Bonny."

"No, it's not possible," Mary was trembling. Her eyes flitted from person to person in the desperate hope that someone would tell her that this was all a joke. "It can't be," she shouted.

"It's all true, Mary," the island matriarch continued, gesturing with her pipe. "Before you were born, your mother was one of the most infamous pirates in the entire Caribbean."

Mary leaped to her feet, her body almost convulsing, and she was gasping in an attempt to capture her breath. Certainly, she had heard about the exploits of the pirate, Anne Bonny. Her eyes flashed between the two women, but since her mouth no longer worked, she simply fled the house. Jack instantly ran after her.

10. The Secret

The next morning Anne and her daughter took a much needed walk together on the beach. Mary had been too flustered the night before for any meaningful conversation, but now calm, she pressed her mother to tell her story. "How did you, a respectable lady, manage to turn pirate in the first place?" Mary asked.

"I grew up on our family plantation; a childhood very similar to yours," Anne began, "Except that my mother died when I was young, and my father raised me much like a boy, which I suppose helped develop a sense of adventure in me. When I was in my twenties, my childhood friend, his name was Jim Bonny, sold his family farm that he had just inherited in order to buy a boat. He wanted to go adventuring in the Bahamas and was planning to sail to Nassau as soon as possible. It sounded so exciting, and I begged him to take me along. Since we had always joked around about how we would marry one day we didn't think it too out of line to ask my father for his permission. Well, not only was your grandfather adamantly against it, but he practically threw poor Jim out of the house. I was so angry that I ran away. That night, Jim and I eloped and we left for The Bahamas on his boat together.

Our troubles began as soon as we arrived in Nassau and found out that the new governor there had granted amnesty to the pirates, and with British warships in the harbor there would be no adventuring for anyone. Jim started running cargo to the other islands, but there was very little money in it, and there was a lot of competition, so I ended up having to get a job serving drinks to make ends meet. It was about that time that I came to realize that I had loved the call of adventure more than I loved Jim, but I was stuck with him there in Nassau.

About a month later I met Mary. She was a pirate who had accepted the amnesty offer, but she'd ran out of money and ended up serving drinks at the same establishment that I was in. She told me all sorts of stories about her colorful past and introduced me to her lover, the infamous pirate Calico Jack Rackham, who had also accepted amnesty and was living large in the city. I've got to tell you, as soon as I laid eyes on him, it was love at first sight for me.

Mary told me how Rackham was having a hard time settling down to civilized life. He was frequently running afoul of the authorities for some reason or another, and that he and some of the other disgruntled pirates, basically those who had spent all of their money, were planning to return to life on the high seas one day. She said that when they did that, she was going to go with him, and she then asked me if I'd like to join them. Of course, I wanted to, but in fairness to Jim I couldn't just run off. After all, I was a married woman. Mary had the perfect answer. She said she noticed how I'd been looking at Jack, and instead of being angry or jealous, she told me that Jack also fancied me, and it was all right with her if we spent some time together. That way I could tell Jim about it and have him divorce me for adultery. Let me tell you, Mary and Jack weren't married, but they were the most secure couple I've ever known, and Jack was an exciting lover.

Anyhow, after a couple of weeks I told Jim about Jack and asked for a divorce, telling him I wanted a new life. He understood, things hadn't worked out for us as we had planned, and he probably figured I was going back home to South Carolina, so we went to the governor together to ask for a divorce decree. Well, the governor refused us. He told me it was my duty as a wife to stay with my husband. I ended up losing my temper and shouted that he had no right to force people to stay married. The governor's response was to order me flogged for adultery.

When Mary and Calico Jack heard what had happened they took me in, and a couple of days later I left with them as a crew member on a their new pirate ship."

"Whew, mother," Mary was impressed. "I never realized you had such a temper."

"Oh yes, it got me into trouble on numerous occasion while I was growing up, but it was also one of the things I was forced to learn to curb later in life."

"So how did you get back from being a pirate and return to a life as a lady on in South Carolina?"

"My pirate days didn't last long; it was just a few months later that we were all captured off Jamaica. When my father found out, he came down to the Caribbean and paid to get me released from jail into his custody. I had to agree to never go to sea again for as long as he lived, and I had to agree to settle down and live an exemplary life as a proper lady. My father also arranged to marry me to James Burleigh, the man who, for all practical purposes, has been your father, as soon as we got back."

"But how could you have kept this from us for all of these years, mother?"

"The only people in South Carolina that ever knew about all of this were my father, your grandfather, who took that secret to the grave with him, and Father Martin at the church, who is sworn to secrecy. Surely you can imagine that it wasn't something I could even begin to tell you or your sisters about, and besides, what good would have become of it?"

"I understand." Mary realized that recent events had put her in a most unique position to be able to appreciate what her mother had gone through.

"And just like I returned to the life I was meant for, so can you, Mary. Just like with my experience, that door is by no means closed to you."

"But I'm not going back, mother. I'm staying here with Jack."

"I don't doubt your feelings and sense of certainty, Mary. But what if it turns out that Jack is just a passing infatuation? Or you are to him? If that happened this lifestyle would rapidly lose its appeal, and you would end up feeling stuck, just like I did with Jim Bonny, and looking for a way out. I just want you to think about it. All right?"

Mary looked sternly at her mother but held back the temptation to lash out. Her feelings for Jack were so strong that it seemed impossible they would ever fade, but at the same time it was true that she had been caught up in a whirlwind, and her mother couldn't be faulted for giving what she believed to be sage advice. Mary simply smiled. Certainly, time spent on the island seeing her and Jack together would surely make her mother realize that these concerns were completely unfounded.

"I do like your mother," Jack told Mary as the two of them were cuddled up in bed that night. "She's definitely a strong woman. But she makes it very clear that she wants you to return to South Carolina with her."

"She certainly has strong opinions, but I wouldn't worry. I've been most insistent with her that I'm not leaving you."

"Oh, she knows how you feel. I think that's why she has been telling me that privateers are being welcomed in the American colonies and regaling me about the pleasures of life as a gentleman."

"She's trying to talk you into going to South Carolina?" Mary sat up and excitedly studied Jack's face. Was he going to consider it?

"Your mother says that all I have to do is accept the king's marque and take on a Spaniard in the southern Caribbean, and I would instantly be considered a hero and considered acceptable in social circles. I would even be considered desirable company and sought out to invite to soirées."

"Well, doesn't that prove that she likes you, too, Jack?"

"I'm not as sure if she likes me as much as she is trying to get me killed and out of the way," Jack laughed. "Pit *The Avenger* against a Spanish galley warship? We'd be blown to pieces." He sat up and gave the bewildered Mary a kiss, then flopped back on the bed. "Your mother is a master manipulator, Mary, but I'm not going to fault her for it. I respect it. But think through what she is saying. If I died fighting the Spanish, I'd go down as a hero, and you could all speak well of me over tea. And if I did survive, she knows a pirate's view on the world well enough. She knows that there is no way I'd be able to endure the hypocrisy of your old lifestyle. So you'd be back on your plantation, for in this scenario you'd go home with her while I go to fight the Spanish, and initially you'd be waiting for me. But as time went by I'd fade into memory, and you would get on with your life. I imagine she would see to that."

"So, what did you tell her?"

"Don't worry," Jack began laughing again when he saw Mary's horrified expression and pulled her down next to him. "I didn't call her on it. I behaved like a gentleman and thanked her for suggesting the opportunity." He kissed Mary on the top of her head. "And all your mother did was simply ask me to think about it."

A week later the captured sloop had been repaired, fitted with a new mast, and was ready to be re-floated. It was decided that since this ship had never been used in piracy, and would therefore have no problems if there were any naval ships in the harbor, it was the perfect vessel to take Anne to Nassau. Plus, the relatively short trip would be a good shake down run to see how she handled. After this trip, it would be re-named and be given to the quartermaster as his command, and then there would then be two pirate ships operating out of Gran Baha, doubling the capacity of the operation. Mary was thrilled to learn that, by a vote of the crew, she was to fill the then vacant quartermaster position on *The Avenger.*

Anne had been unsuccessful in swaying her daughter to even consider returning with her to South Carolina, but since the Maries had otherwise thoroughly enjoyed spending time with her, she asked both of them to go with her to Nassau where they could do some shopping together in the capital city before she went home. Jack elected to remain on the island, agreeing it would be good for the three women to continue to spend time together. He was confident that with his mother close by, Mary would be safe from Anne's expected last minute coercive tactics.

There were high spirits all around when Jack gave Mary a goodbye kiss, and the two of them promised they would be together again in just a few days.

Mary Read took the captain's cabin with Anne and Mary joining her there for meals. Discussion had remained light throughout the trip with Anne making no mention of Mary returning with her to the colonies, but with the ship due to arrive in Nassau the next morning, Anne predictably brought up the inevitable at dinner that night.

"I've told you quite repeatedly, mother." Mary said with controlled politeness. "I have no intention of going back with you. My life is now with Jack."

"I was hoping I wasn't going to have to tell you this," Anne responded slowly, "but you really need to hear the full story about my pirate days before you make that a final decision." She swallowed hard and tried to not look into the two pairs of eyes boring into her. "Mary here can vouch for the truth of what I'm about to say."

"I can't imagine how anything you have to say will change things, mother."

"This will," Anne snapped back. "Don't patronize me, young lady." She took a deep breath, exhaled through her mouth and continued.

"What I didn't tell you about when I went off to sea with Jack Rackham and Mary is that the three of us shared the bed in his cabin."

Mary was incredulous. "You mean, the two of you?" she wagged her finger between them.

"Oh, it wasn't like the two us of together if that's what you're thinking," Anne laughed, "But Mary and I did share Calico Jack?" Anne smiled. In spite of the nature of the discussion they were having, this was clearly a long suppressed happy memory for her and she was relishing in the re-living of it.

"There was no jealousy or anything," Mary Read chimed in. "All three of us were simply caught up in a time of incredible passion."

"Anyhow," Anne shook herself to regain composure. "On the voyage back to South Carolina, after my father came and got me and I started to throw up, he realized I was pregnant, so I was married off really quickly so my child would be born respectably." She grabbed hold of her daughter's hands. "That child was you, Mary."

Mary violently shook her hands free and erratically flailed them about. "No, no, no," she shouted, then leaped up from the table, ran to the corner of the room and vomited into a bucket. "How could you not tell me," she sobbed. "How could you let me continue to be with him when you knew he was my brother?"

"I'm so sorry, Mary." Anne wrapped her arm around her daughter and handed her a cloth to wipe her face on.

Mary stood up, still in her mother's embrace, and the two of them then went back to the table and sat down again.

"So Jack is your half-brother," Mary Read began brightly. "I don't see what the problem is." She raised her hands, about to explain further, but Mary slammed her fist onto the table.

"We're still related," Mary barked out through her sniffles. "It's not natural."

"Royalty brothers and sisters marry all the time, you know." Mary Read looked first at Mary, then at Anne. "And there's no law against half siblings marrying," she continued but quickly realized from their expressions that there was no use in persisting so she fell silent.

"I'll write a letter to Jack telling him that I realized my home is in the colonies, that I had to return to it, and to tell him to forget me," Mary blubbered. "But you have to promise me something," Mary desperately squeezed Mary Read's hand into hers. "Please, please never let Jack now that we have the same father. Never, ever, ever." She was screaming, but she managed to calm herself with a deep breath. "I can't bear for him to know that he bedded his sister." Her bawling overcame her, and Jack's mother put her arm around Mary's convulsing body to console her. "I promise, Mary," she whispered. "He'll never know."

Mary settled to a simple sniffling, but a sudden thought came over her, and she quickly turned to her mother. "Who else knows about this?" She demanded.

"Nobody but us three," Anne replied softly. "Just us."

The ship was already docked in Nassau when Mary awoke, surprised that she had slept so soundly after drenching the pillow with her tears the night before. She and her mother said their goodbyes and debarked into the bustle of the busy port and began to walk into town when Mary stopped and said, "I'm really not in the mood to go shopping, mother. Why don't we just see about arranging for passage home?"

"That's simple enough," Anne replied. "*The Anne* is docked somewhere around here, it's waiting for us." She turned to her daughter's glare. "Don't you dare to look at me like that, young lady. Did you really believe I was about to stay in the Bahamas without arranging for a way back for us? I had Captain Fordham sail here to wait for us as soon as I went off with you to meet Jack."

"You had this all planned out, didn't you?"

"But of course I did, my dear. What mother would let her child ruin her life like that? It was my hope you would have come to see reason on your own, but unfortunately, your obstinance prevented that.

I truly am sorry it had to come to this, but if that was the only means to convince you to return home with me, so be it." Anne sighed a contained sigh of satisfaction. She had Mary returning with her as she wanted, but it would have not been appropriate for Mary to see her mother smiling just then.

11. Privateers

Following three days of antisocial drunkenness, Jack sat down in his house and re-read the now tattered letter that his mother had brought back from Nassau. Angry as he was, if anger was the right term for what he was feeling, he kept trying to read between the lines to understand why. What was the tipping point that led Mary to leave him like this? The most plausible explanation, he concluded, was that Anne must have used a variation of the same approach on her daughter that she had tried to use on him. She must have convinced Mary that, if Jack truly loved her, then he would leave his life of piracy and join her in her world of wealth and luxury. Anne must have convinced Mary that only by leaving him would Jack have sufficient incentive to act nobly, to take the king's marque and become both rich and a hero; the requirements for him to enter their world as a gentleman. Anne undoubtedly would have added that if Jack did not pursue this course, it would be because he either didn't really love Mary or that he was a coward. This would also explain, then, why Mary ended her letter by telling him to live his life without her. She knew Jack was certainly not a coward, but she didn't want him to be in harm's way either, so she tried to take away the reason for doing so by saying she was no longer available to him.

"All right then," Jack growled loudly and picked up one of the bottles of rum from the table. He pulled the cork out with his teeth, spat it across the room, and chugged back a third of the sweet, dark liquid that had recently made up the biggest part of his diet. "We'll play it your way." He stumbled outside and meandered his way to the beach taking swigs along the way. Now that he knew what he had to do if he wanted get Mary back, he had to figure out if he could really go about doing it. He sat down on the sand and stared at The Avenger anchored just off shore. Fighting the Spanish didn't bother him; his sloop was faster upwind than any warship, so as long as he carefully picked the angle of a fight, he could always beat away if things went wrong. He took another guzzle of his rum. "Love or principles?" he questioned into the ever present island breeze. Jack knew his biggest issue was going to be whether he would be able to live in a so called civilized world. Was he willing and able give up that much of himself in order to be with Mary? He cursed the fact that he hadn't followed the lessons his mother had drilled into him about never falling in love, drained the bottle, and fell flat backwards onto the beach.

Everyone anxiously piled into the meeting room the following afternoon to hear what Jack had to say. He hadn't even told his mother about his plan. He stood tall in front of the crowded room, sober, clean shaven, and resplendent in his blue silk jacket and polished leather boots; nothing like the despondent drunk that everybody had become used to over the past week. "As you all know," he began, "Mary Burleigh has returned to South Carolina. Through her mother, I have been offered the opportunity to join her."

A shocked gasp reverberated through the hall, but no one said anything.

"What is first required, however, is that I become a respectable and wealthy gentleman, which I can do by turning privateer and capturing a substantial quantity of Spanish gold. My only chance of pulling this off is with the best crew in the Bahamas, the crew of The Avenger, but I can't in good conscience ask any of you to join me without telling you the risks. We'll not be taking cargo from merchants on this trip; we'll be attacking Spaniards, and they won't be likely to just hand their treasure over to us. There will be real fighting, there are going to be casualties, and some of you that choose to go may not be returning. Those that do make it back, though, are going to be rich; rich enough to never have to go pirating again. Who wants to join me?"

The quartermaster immediately stood up. "Beg your pardon, captain, but before the crew can vote to do this with you, we're going to need to know how is it that we're going to end up so rich? The British have hundreds of privateers in action between Cuba and the Windward Islands, yet none of us have heard tell of any of those lads gettin' out of there with huge riches."

"That's because we're not going to join them in the theater of war." Jack clenched his right fist and grinned. "After we leave Jamaica with our marque, we're going to sail south, right towards the Spanish Main. You see, the Spanish turn the gold from the South American mines into coinage at their mint in Cartagena, and from there a ship goes out every two months carrying the payroll for the entire Spanish Caribbean fleet. The target I want us to go after is that payroll ship."

"What do you know about this ship, cap'n?" The quartermaster was decidedly interested. "How well armed is she?"

"She's a 250 ton frigate and carries twenty two guns." Jack paused to let the sounds of gasping subside. "But we have two sloops now, ships that can outpoint and outrun a frigate upwind, and without us carrying any cargo we can refit them both to each carry two more guns. That'll put our ships at ten guns apiece. It'll be a fight, no doubt about it, but my thinking is that we have a damn good shot at pulling this off."

Jack finished his presentation by asking if there were any questions before he called for a vote, but the quartermaster stood up and interrupted him. He asked Jack to leave the meeting hall so the crew could discuss it amongst themselves without his influence. Since this was completely contradictory to their way of pirating, he wanted each man to be free to say what he really thought about it. The quartermaster would then bring it to a vote and let Jack know their decision without revealing who voted which way.

Jack agreed, donned his tricorn and left the meeting. He began to walk towards the beach when his mother rushed up from behind him. "What's wrong with you, Jack?" She admonished. "You've just asked your crew to risk their lives so you can end up leaving them for a life you can't possibly want."

"It's not about that life, mother. It's about being with Mary."

"Of course it's about Mary," she choked as she shouted at him. "But don't you think you're being way too selfish here? I can see you don't care if you get yourself killed, but these men look up to you and you're responsible for them."

"I told them the risks." Jack continued walking.

"Look at yourself, hell bent for fame and glory. I've seen battle, Jack. Men get killed and maimed in horrible ways." She grabbed hold of the front of Jack's jacket with her right hand to make him stand still and pointed back to the town hall. "Go back inside right now and tell them it's too dangerous, Jack. Let us keep our life the way we have it."

Jack grabbed his mother's hand and pulled it away. "I'm going to do this, mother." Jack was calmly matter-of-fact. He smoothed the front of his jacket. "And I'm not going to force anyone to go with me. These men know the risks, so if they decide to join me, it will be on them. If they don't want to, I'll just take my ship to Nassau or Jamaica where there are plenty of sailors who will. I'm going to get rich and win Mary back or die in the trying, and right now either option is just fine with me."

"Please, Jack, please don't do this. You're upset now, and that's understandable. Just give it time. You'll get over her and everything will be all right again before you know it; you'll see."

Jack was about to explain how it was not his intention to get over Mary, but their conversation was interrupted by Jermy rushing up to him. "Capt'n, sah, the vote's took an' I wuz tol' me to cum fetch ya, sah."

Jack half smiled at his mother and rushed back to the town hall, took a deep breath and then walked inside without removing his hat. He stood erect and expressionless in front of the assembly, feet twelve inches apart and arms at his sides, and silently waited for the verdict. The quartermaster, his face giving nothing away, rose from his seat and stood next to him. "The crew has said, aye, cap'n."

"Thank you quartermaster," Jack replied matter-of-factly, forcing himself to conceal his delight. He removed his hat, and now visibly more relaxed than he had been since before the meeting began, added, "I thank you all. As you know, this is personal for me, but the rewards for all of us if we achieve success will be substantial."

"Three cheers for the captain," someone in the crowd shouted out.

Hands on his hips, Jack grinned at his mother standing at the back of the room as his crew boisterously cheered their leader.

"Tell me, quartermaster," Jack asked. "Have you come up with a name for your new command?"

"Indeed I have, captain," The quartermaster grinned, "On account of how we came by her, I'm calling her *Rumrunner*."

"Then let's toast to it," Jack added loudly, "Friends, I give you Captain Richard King of the sloop, *Rumrunner*. Let's have rum all around."

Work began immediately on fitting each ship with an additional gun port on each side, and all the extra sails and rigging they had on shore were loaded into the cargo holds along with gunpowder and provisions. They would buy four more cannons while in Jamaica and recruit additional crew while there. The ships so configured would be as formidable as any naval sloop of war.

In the meeting before they left, Jack made sure that everyone was aware of the secrecy of their mission and not to discuss it with anyone while they were ashore in Jamaica. "As far as anyone in Port Royal is to know," Jack told them, "Once we get our marque we'll be privateers sailing under the king's colors along the shipping lanes in and around Puerto Rico."

As luck had it, Jack didn't even have to purchase the cannons. While in the Windward Passage, they encountered a brig flying French colors heading towards Hispaniola which refused to heave to when ordered and instead fired on the *Rumrunner*. While Captain King kept her engaged, *The Avenger* maneuvered to close range and fired a deadly volley of grapeshot across the deck, effectively clearing it of most of the crew. Half of the brig's riggings were blown away, and the forward mast toppled and crashed down into the deck. Jack ordered both sloops to close in and board.

The remaining French were outnumbered, but their captain nevertheless refused to ask for quarter. None of them survived the relatively short battle; those who hadn't been killed by the grapeshot volley from *The Avenger's* cannons were shot by pistols before they were even in cutlass range.

The captured brig was then sailed a short distance and beached on nearby Seal Cay. Two cannons each were transferred to *The Avenger* and *Rumrunner* along with all of the shot and powder that was on board. The doomed ship was then set alight before the pirates left to continue on to the British naval headquarters in Jamaica. The two ships working in unison had proved to be a highly effective combination, and this victory served as a splendid bolster to the crew who knew there was going to be this type of fighting in their near future.

Obtaining a letter of marque required nothing more than taking a pledge of loyalty to King George and having an armed ship with an able bodied crew. The British were short of official naval vessels, and those were primarily engaged in repeated attempts to take the city of Havana, so in order to effectively confront the Spanish and disrupt their trade as much as possible throughout the Caribbean, the crown needed every privateer craft they could muster and simply chose not to inquire about the backgrounds of the captain and the crew. When

The Avenger and *Rumrunner* sailed into the Port Royal harbor it was obvious to the authorities that these were pirate vessels, but two ten gunners keen to join the fight against the Spanish were well received, and the officer in command provided them with letters of marque and gave them their Union Jacks without question. Besides, pirates came with the reputation of being good fighters.

Jack and the two ships left the naval base at Port Royal flying the king's colors and sailed along the Jamaican coast to Kingston for shore leave and to recruit more crew, selecting only those applicants with battle experience. Two days later and with an additional twelve men on board *The Avenger* and fifteen more on *Rumrunner*, the ships set sail heading south for a fortnight of open sea, directly towards the heart of the Spanish Main.

12. Solution

Mary refused to leave her cabin on *The Anne* for the majority of the voyage from Nassau to South Carolina, and so the first opportunity Anne had to speak to her daughter was when they left Charleston and were obliged to sit together in the carriage for the journey back to the plantation. Mary sat brusquely and refused to even look at her mother, feigning preoccupation with the passing countryside.

"I do know how your feel, you know, Mary" Anne told her. "When my father brought me back from Jamaica, I was depressed too. I missed the islands and the man I thought, at least at the time, that I loved. His name was even Jack, too."

Mary slowly turned her face from staring out of the window and glared at Anne. She had made no attempt to conceal her agitation with her mother ever since they left the Bahamas, and Anne, now trying to make their situations analogous, was absolutely infuriating to her. "There is a huge difference, Mother." Mary annunciated each word loudly as she spoke to emphasize that fact. "When you were brought back here, your Jack, Jack Rackham, was dead. You undoubtedly went through a period of mourning and were subsequently able to resume your life here, but there can be no such cure for what I've lost. How can I mourn for a man whom I know to be very much alive? A perfect man who, because of my being forced to tell a lie to, most likely thinks I callously discarded him and ran away." Mary inhaled deeply in an attempt to control her quivering lower lip. "So you see, Mother, unlike you, I'm condemned to a lifetime of pining for what can never be again." Mary quickly turned and stared out of the window again. "So, please," her voice broke down. "Just leave me alone."

Anne sat silently for close to five minutes before gingerly sliding her right hand onto Mary's left shoulder. "Of course, I'll do as you wish and not bring the subject up again, Mary. Just know I'm always here and have your best interests at heart."

There was no response.

"Treat me in this way if you will," Anne continued. "But you do realize that Joseph and your sisters are going to be overjoyed to see you when we arrive at home, don't you? Is it your intention to be so unfriendly towards them as well?"

"Just tell them I am tired or not feeling well or whatever you want. I don't care. I just don't want to have to talk to anybody." Mary turned her head and jutted her chin towards her mother and slowly added a forced smile devoid of sincerity. "You'll have no problem convincing them since you know so well about how I feel."

Joseph's ebullience and her sister's smiles and hugs as soon as Mary climbed out of the carriage were contagious, and for a while it seemed that she may even smile herself, but the excitement of homecoming was temporary and the feeling soon faded. After dinner that night, Mary went to her bedroom and gave in to deep depression. For more than six weeks, when not sequestered in her room, she moped around the house, showed no interest in doing anything that her family members suggested, and insisted that resuming her duties of assisting Joseph with the plantation management was, "Completely out of the question." Mary even refused to even go outside; the walks that she had loved so much in the past offered no appeal at all to her. It was Cynthia, Mary's youngest sister, who finally shook her out of her slump.

Returning from a trip into town, Cynthia excitedly rushed up to the couch Mary was sprawled out on and plopped down next to her.

"What was the name of your pirate captain, Mary?" She asked, teasingly waving a news bulletin above her head. "It wasn't Jack Read, was it?"

"Yes, that is his name." Mary sat bolt upright. "Why? What do you have there?"

"It's the latest news about the war from Port Royal. It seems that a British warship was losing a battle with a Spaniard when two fast fighting sloops, British privateers, came to its aid and not only saved the warship but actually sank the Spanish man o' war. It says here that the ship leading the attack was called *The Avenger* and its captain, Jack Read, is being called Britain's newest naval hero."

Mary snatched the paper, and gripping it tightly in her trembling hands read it over and over again. "My god, he's really doing it," she muttered, then handed the paper back her sister and leaped to her feet.

"What do you mean?" Cynthia was shocked by this sudden burst of activity.

Mary didn't answer her sister's question, instead blurting out that she was going outside for a walk and tore out through the front doorway. Her head was spinning; the only reason Jack would have gone privateer was to legitimize himself so he could come to South Carolina, to come and find her.

"What if he does come for me?" Mary spoke thoughtfully into the cool breeze as she revisited her favorite childhood haunts, once again enjoying the feel of the sun on her now pallid face. The possibility of seeing Jack again was all she could think about. But if he did come to the plantation, he would have to be told that they were brother and sister, and what then? Mary recalled her horror she felt when her mother told this terrible secret, but then she also recollected how Mary Read hadn't seen it as an issue at all. That was it; Jack's mother had tried to tell them that sibling marriages must be allowed because royalty do it all the time. It was her own preconception that prevented Mary from paying due attention to this oh so wise woman.

Mary rushed back to the house to the family library and quickly found the book she needed: The Forbidden Marriage Laws. It was a text which had been drawn up by the Church of England in 1560 and had ever since been the ultimate authority on the subject. She stood next to the table in the middle of the room, opened the book to the index, and fingers as awkward as thumbs, fumbled to the page she wanted and rapidly scanned down the list. Her heart sank when she reached number sixteen where it specifically stated that a brother and sister could not marry. Deflated, Mary sank into a chair, but, nevertheless, continued to look over the list because she was now curious about the many relationships that were listed; there were thirty in all. Nieces, nephews and in-laws were all forbidden from marrying. But then in the explanatory wording that came after the list, it stated that since stepbrothers and stepsisters had been excluded they were therefore permitted to marry. "Well then," Mary whispered to herself. While she and Jack were not step siblings, they weren't full brother and sister either. They were, in fact, half siblings with each having different mothers. And half siblings were not on the list. Mary's excitement returned and she rose again from the chair. With a list that inclusive, she reasoned, surely half siblings would be on it if they were not allowed to marry. She slammed the book shut, picked it up in both hands and beamed while tapping it onto her chin. Everything was going to be all right now. Jack was going to come for her, and there was no impediment to them being together.

Mary went outside again and smiled up into the bright spring sunshine. Soon it would be planting season. She would busy herself assisting with the plantation management to make the time go quickly by until Jack arrived. She set about to find Joseph, the man she had always known as her father. She would always call him that. Neither he nor Mary's sisters had been told of her mother's shameful secret, and Mary was delighted that it was to remain that way.

Joseph never asked what finally prompted Mary out of her slump. After the family had made so many fruitless attempts, he was simply thrilled to have her back to her old self. Over the past decade he had come to depend on her help in managing the plantation, and her expertise would have been especially missed at this busy time of year.

During her depression Mary had been oblivious to the house slaves and had given no thought to how her attitude towards slavery had been adjusted during her time with Jack, but when she first laid eyes on Jethro after Joseph had called him to a meeting, she felt an unexpected surge of guilt. "Hello Jethro," she said quietly.

"Oh, it be soo good ta see ya again, Miz Mary," Jethro almost bellowed back at her.

"I must tell you, Jethro, that you were right. There were pirates in the Bahamas."

"I'm so sorry fer bein' right, Miz Mary." He looked down and slowly shook his head from side to side, but then his head sprang up again sporting a toothy grin. "But weeze all glad ya made it back home all in one piece."

"How are the new fields shaping up Jethro," Joseph asked.

"All the canals and the levees and the dams are all ready, Mister Joseph, and so the field slaves can start wiv the plantin soon. A couple of 'em got snake bites and laid up right now, but they'll be ready for work agin in a few days. I reckon ta have all the field slaves out sowin' rice next week, and then I can flood them fields Easter week."

"Splendid, Jethro," Joseph said as he stood up and dismissed him. He turned to Mary. "We're really too reliant on that old slave, you know," he told her. "We still need to get a couple of younger planters in here. Too bad those damn pirates stole the two you'd bought; Captain Fordham told me they were a couple of exceptional bucks. I'll bet those blighters sold them right back to some unscrupulous trader."

"Actually," Mary suppressed her anger by controlling her breathing as she spoke, remembering that not too long ago she would have probably said the same thing. "They were offered a chance to join the pirates, and both became valuable members of the ship's crew."

"Uncivilized louts, the lot of them." Joseph was incredulous.

After seeing Jethro and now remembering how Willum and Jermy had become her friends on the island, Mary realized just how much she had changed over the previous few months, and it was suddenly obvious that she was going to be unable to reconcile with slavery. The slaves, at least those with education, were fellow human beings. Perhaps she could deceive herself into overlooking the use of field slaves who didn't speak English because they had no other options; they were provided food and lodging in exchange for their labor which may be considered somewhat equitable. But those with skills must certainly not be treated as property.

"It seems to me, father," Mary picked her words thoughtfully, "That Jethro is really much more than a slave?"

"Indeed he is. If he were a white man with such skills as he has, he could command a small fortune. He basically runs the operation. That's why it is so important for us to have a backup in case something happens to him."

"Don't you think, then, it would be fairer to pay him what he is worth?"

"What are you talking about, Mary? We don't have to pay him because we own him, so how does fair enter into that? He is our slave, our property."

"When I was with the pirates, I saw everybody treated equally, and there were no slaves. Why not give Jethro his freedom, and then hire him as the overseer?"

"That's a good one, Mary," Joseph's laughter, while quite genuine, was infuriating. "I take it that's a bit of island humor, eh?"

"But he is a skilled human being, father. It isn't right that we keep him as property."

"Actually," Joseph wiped his eyes with his right hand and then slid his fingers down his face to extinguish his mirth. "I do see what you are saying, and I could even agree with you in principal, but that's the sort of talk that could bankrupt us." He shook his head. "Plantations are a competitive business. They survive on slave labor, Mary, and that's the end of it."

"Perhaps it is," Mary thought as she set about the books. Clearly, she was unlikely to find a way to turn things around on her own, so she would have to suck it up and live with it until Jack arrived. If Jack couldn't figure out how to make money in the civilized world without the use of slaves, then neither of them were going to be able to remain here.

Unlike Joseph, Anne was most curious as to what it was that so miraculously transformed Mary, and so she asked her daughter point blank.

"Did you see the news report about Jack that Cynthia brought home?" Mary said in response to her mother's query.

"I did." Anne replied. "He took the king's marque and is making quite a name for himself. Of course, that's only to be expected since he is Calico Jack's son."

"The only reason he would have gone privateer is because you told him that was the only way he could be with me. This means he intends to come here."

"But if he does, Mary, won't that make things even worse for you? Nothing has changed about the fact that you're brother and sister."

"Ah, but that's where we made a wrong assumption, Mother. I should have listened to Mary Read when she said that since Jack and I are only half siblings, it would be all right for us to marry. I checked, and according to the law, she was right. We are able to after all."

Mary went on to explain her research and the rationale behind her conclusion. Anne was genuinely pleased for her, but while hopeful that Mary was correct, she doubted that such a wishful solution could be true. Rather than even sew a seed of doubt, though, she joined Mary in her enthusiasm, and the two of them sat down and enjoyed a pot of tea together for the first time since they had been with Mary Read.

Anne had been quite effective in suppressing her skepticism in order to be able to spend some pleasant time with Mary but all the while they sat together, her doubt continued to well up inside. It took her to the point that when tea was over, she immediately left the house and went into town to seek out Father Martin for final clarification.

"My family has been having an ongoing discussion about what types of relations are able to marry each other, and we are unresolved about half brothers and sisters," Anne began. "The Forbidden Marriage Laws does not specifically list them, and in the explanatory notes it suggests that anything not listed is allowed. One of my daughters interprets this to mean that half brothers and sisters are to be treated in the same manner as step siblings and be allowed to marry, but the others disagree with her. Since we are unable to resolve it ourselves, I've come to you to ask for a church ruling on the matter."

Father Martin slowly shook his head from side to side. "Half brother and sister are blood relatives," he said. "So in the eyes of the church, and the law, they are the same full siblings and may not marry."

"That was all of our original understandings too, Father. But then Mary suggested that since these types of marriages occur frequently within the royal houses of Europe, then it must be permissible."

"Ah! You may tell Mary that while her assumption does follow the rules of logic, she begins with the false premise that royals are ordinary people. Royalty are appointed by God, and the mortal rules of marriage do not apply to them. A king, for instance, may marry whomever he so desires, even his sister, if he wishes it. A common person may not."

"I see." Anne nodded. "Thank you for the clarification, this all makes sense to me now."

Anne walked slowly back to the plantation from the church agonizing as to whether she should tell Mary that her interpretation of the marriage laws had been flawed, but by the time she arrived home she had concluded that it was best to just keep quiet about it. It was wonderful that Mary was no longer depressed, and even if Jack's intention were to come to South Carolina, he was up against long odds of survival in the Caribbean at the moment. There was really no sense in upsetting her daughter with this because chances were very good that Jack was never going to make it.

13. Battle

Jack was not the only person to have heard about the payroll shipments from the Spanish Main. The British Navy also had designs on the payroll ship, and had sent a 30 gun warship to intercept it and bring the chests of reales and doubloons back to Port Royal.

While the British attempted to keep the plan secret, well placed Spanish spies in Port Royal had learned of it and sent word back to Cartagena even before the warship had left the naval headquarters. This had enabled the Spanish to prepare, and they sent a heavily armed escort ship out a day ahead of the payroll ship to take out the British vessel first. The Spanish man o' war was a 500 ton ship rigged frigate with 40 guns on two decks, a floating fortress which would have annihilated the two privateer sloops had they run into it.

Fortunately for the privateers, by the time *The Avenger* and *Rumrunner* came across the two warships, the battle had already been raging for the biggest part of a day, and both craft had suffered a great deal of damage in the process. The Spaniard had the upper hand when they intercepted them; the British vessel was being overwhelmed and attempting to break free of the engagement. *The Avenger* and *Rumrunner* raised their Union Jacks, and moving to aid the British warship, attacked in a line formation, swiftly running up the starboard side of the Spaniard from the aft and hitting it with a double broadside while the British ship rejoined the fight and bombarded it on the port. The sloops then made a quick tack and struck the Spaniard on the same side that they had just hit with their starboard batteries. Rapidly taking on water, the man o' war listed to starboard and began to sink. She struck her colors in surrender, and the British warship lowered boats into the water to pick up the survivors.

The Avenger and *Rumrunner* heaved to alongside each other, and Jack ordered a boat be dropped to row him and Captain King across to the British ship. A rope ladder was rolled down as they approached, and after receiving an invitation to board, they clambered up it. On the deck were two perfect rows of sailors who snapped to attention as the captains were piped aboard, and Jack whispered to his comrade not to laugh as they sauntered between them. They were welcomed by Captain Horne and two of his officers at the end of the receiving line.

"Captain Jack Read of the privateer *The Avenger* and Captain Richard King of the *Rumrunner* at your service, Captain," Jack responded respectfully.

"My compliments, captains." Captain Horne took a step forward and extended his hand to shake theirs. "That was a fine display of valor and seamanship. You will both receive my highest commendations for your service. Please join me and my officers in my cabin for refreshment."

Nobody mentioned the payroll ship while they feasted on roast beef and washed it down with navy rum. In fact, it was the quality of the rum that dominated much of the discussion, and the English captain, delighting in the sophisticated palate of his guests, presented each of them with a small keg of it before they returned to their ships.

After the requisite meeting with Captain's Read and King had been concluded, Captain Horne and the victorious British warship sailed back to Jamaica to deliver the prisoners of war and to make repairs. Never mind the glory that the much hailed incident of two heroic privateers going to the aid of a British warship brought them, the net result of this incident proved to be much more important for Jack and his crew. Not only had the British ship been crucial in eliminating the threat of the Spanish warship, but the damage it sustained was going to force it to remain in Port Royal where it would be out of action for several months, ensuring that it could not possibly interfere with Jack and his fellow privateers' designs on the Spanish payroll ship.

Two days later, the lookout on *The Avenger* sighted sails coming head on across the southern horizon. Jack immediately called for the two privateers to heave to, and Captain Richard King swung aboard from *Rumrunner* to confer with him.

"Well Jack," the former quartermaster stood with his hands on his hips and sporting a huge grin on his grizzled face. "I've got to hand it to you, you've got us through almost 600 miles of Spanish waters, and we're still all in one piece. So, tell me now, what's your plan for how we're going to go about takin' this treasure?"

"The payroll ship's beating into the easterlies which is bound to be giving a ship like that a good heel, so if we run up on each side of her, we can use that to minimize our damage. You take *Rumrunner* out at full range on the lee and fire chain and grapeshot onto her deck and into her rigging while I take *The Avenger* close in to windward, and I'll blast her starboard gun deck. You'll be high out of range of her port guns, and hopefully, we'll be low enough to take most of 'em out on her starboard while their shot goes over our heads. Then you'll come around and close in, and both crews will board from her starboard side."

"I like it, Jack.' Richard rubbed his chin. "That Spaniard's main guns are most likely to be 32 pounders, and our biggest are 24s. We'd be sure to lose out if it comes to a prolonged sea battle, so the sooner we get to fighting on her deck the better."

"What's the mood amongst the crew, Richard?"

"Oh, they're all ready for it. Every last man is right now dreaming of riches and glory."

"That's good to hear." Jack made a strong affirmative nod. "We might all be in this for ourselves, that's how it should be, but this time it's going to be different to anything we've been up against in the past. We've had a few skirmishes before, but merchants usually give up quickly, and we lucked out against the French. Today, though, we're flying King George's flag, so today we are the British engaging the Spanish. This is a military style conflict, and none of us have ever been in a fight to the death battle against a well-armed enemy before."

"Then here's hoping my first volley does the job of clearing the deck, then. Eh, Jack?"

The two privateers sailed an intercept course bearing down on the Spanish vessel while the crews readied themselves for the upcoming battle. Jack dressed in his cabin, donning his familiar silk jacket and tricorn hat, and then went out on deck to receive his weaponry from the bosun. Cutlass swaying at his side and two loaded pistols tucked in his belt, he marched the length of the ship in a show of encouragement for his crew and then stood alone at the prow. The Spaniard was less than half a mile ahead of *The Avenger* now, and they were closing on her fast. He removed his hat with his right hand and looked up to the bowsprit letting the wind blow through his hair and feeling the salt spray on his face as his sloop cut through the waves. "Well Mary," he said into the wind, standing upright and holding onto the rail with his left hand. "By the end of this day I'll either be rich and coming for you, or else I'll be dead. Either way, my problem is about to be solved." He took in a deep breath, put his hat back on, and walked back to stand over the main deck. "Helm," he bellowed. "Ten degrees to starboard and take us alongside close. Gun crews stand ready on the port side." He looked to the left making sure *Rumrunner* was properly positioned, then resumed his post at the port bow and grabbed onto a rope ladder. There were only hundred yards to go.

Suddenly the Spanish vessel veered to port which not only moved it closer to *Rumrunner*, but more disturbing, moved it from a beat to a reach at which point it began to level out, destroying the privateer's advantage.

"Hard to port," Jack shouted as their quarry began to move away. Being a faster boat, *The Avenger* was still able catch up and get alongside. Jack waited until they were positioned under the Spaniard's gun deck before calling out, "Fire." The enemy fired all its guns at the same time and disappeared into the ensuing clouds of acrid smoke while cannonballs screamed close overhead and tore through *The Avenger's* sails and rigging. The helmsman screamed, "Look out below," as the top half of the mast crashed onto the deck. Jack looked up he saw a crosspar of the enemy ship moving over him. The ships were drifting together, lost in the smoke. "Grappling hooks," he yelled. "All crew to port. Prepare to board." They were dead in the water and without maneuverability; their only option was to latch onto the enemy vessel. The hulls of the two ships were less than ten feet away from each other and the main crosspars of the enemy were about to rip out what was left of *The Avenger's* upper rig. Any distance between the ships would have made *The Avenger* a sitting duck for the Spanish guns, but at close quarters like this they had a chance.

The wind rapidly cleared the smoke as twenty grappling hooks snagged onto the rail of the Spaniard, and the crew threw nets across and set about securing the two boats together. Jack jumped up onto the rail of *The Avenger*, ready to swing across to lead the boarding party, when suddenly there was a row of Spanish marines armed with muskets. "Hit the deck," he screamed. Seconds later a musket ball blew the tricorn from his head as he dove down to the safety of the ships deck, then leaped back to his feet and shouted out, "Follow me quick lads; don't let them reload."

Half the crew swung across on ropes while the rest scrambled over using the nets. "Pistols at the quick," Jack ordered as they attacked the marines who had fallen back to reload. Half of them got shots off before the privateers' volley mowed them down, but five of Jack's men also fell. "Draw cutlasses and stay together." Jack yelled. He could hear Captain King's voice bellowing behind them and knew that reinforcements were on their way over. "Hold position."

The Spanish seamen surged towards them, but Jack's party had the advantage with the rail at their backs, and they were soon joined by the boarding party from *Rumrunner* who, with fresh pistols, were able to stop a dozen Spaniards from even getting into sword range. The bloodshed was both terrible and exhilarating at the same time. His own men were falling, but Jack called for them to press ahead, and wildly swinging his cutlass at anything that moved, lead the way aft in hopes of finding the captain. With his marines gone and so many of his crew dead, the privateers most likely now outnumbered them. Surely he would surrender rather than allow this carnage to continue.

"English captain," A voice boomed out from up at the rail in front of the helm. Jack looked up to see a tall man dressed in a purple and gold uniform with his sword drawn coming down the stairs toward him. "Come meet me if you dare."

"Call for surrender, captain," Jack answered. "And I'll grant you and your crew quarter."

"One of us is about die with honor, captain. I will not be asking for quarter."

"Then none shall be given." Jack lunged forward and the captains' swords crossed with them midway on the staircase. The Spaniard was clearly the better swordsman, but it was Jack's unbridled bloodlust that won the day as, oblivious to the pain from the wound he had received to his left arm, he rushed into his opponent and knocked him to the ground, then stood above him and hacked him to death.

There were four large chests in the Spanish captain's cabin; two were filled with gold doubloons, and the other two with silver pieces of eight. This was more treasure than the privateers had ever seen. Even after the British authorities took their half, they would still be left with more than any of them could have ever imagined. Jack had been true to his word; his men had followed him as he had asked, and now they were about to be rich as he had promised.

Jack had also told them that some of them may not survive, but even he had not anticipated the weight of this cost. Twenty nine of the crew had been killed in the action and sixteen were injured, five of them so badly they were out of commission.

The Avenger had lost the top half of her mast, a third of the sails were shredded, and her rigging was a shambles.

The situation aboard *Rumrunner* was worse. The Spaniard's broadside had hit her just above the waterline, and in spite of quick repairs by the gun crew, she was continuing to take on water. So long as the pumps were manned full time and there was no rough weather, they would be able to keep ahead of it, but she needed to make port in order to affect proper repairs.

Jack and Richard received the damage reports while sitting on the chests in the fallen Spanish captain's office. "We'll have to split up, and each ship will have to fend for herself," Jack began. "It's the only way. You need to get *Rumrunner* to dry dock as fast as possible, and the closest friendly port to here is Port Royal. You can be there in ten days by yourself; it would take *The Avenger* nigh on a month at best in the condition that she's in. Take the badly wounded with you."

"But I can't leave you dead in the water, Jack. When this payroll ship doesn't show up in a week or so, the Spanish are going to come looking for her."

"I can get *The Avenger* patched up and I'll get us out here, don't you worry. But it's only a matter of time before a storm blows in, and if you're caught in rough weather, there'll be no way you'll be able to save *Rumrunner*. In the meantime, just to be safe," Jack slapped the side of the chest he was sitting on. "We'll split this booty between our two ships." He grinned and rocked back and forth and waited until his old quartermaster's eyes suddenly became large indicating he understood what Jack meant before adding, "That way the authorities will be kept satisfied."

Two chests were each taken aboard the privateer sloops and the crews were rearranged. All of those who had been taken on in Jamaica were put aboard *Rumrunner*, along with anyone who was in need of medical attention. Jack on *The Avenger* was left with fifteen of his original crew. *Rumrunner* then left for Port Royal while Jack's crew scavenged the payroll ship for whatever might be useful to them, and then scuttled her.

The good fortune of calm weather and favorable winds enabled *Rumrunner* to arrive in the Port Royal harbor in just over a week, and after reporting to the naval authorities, Captain King was given the well-earned commission of half of the treasure they brought with them, minus a charge for repairs to his ship. Since equal shares rightfully belonged to Jack and the remainder of the crew on *The Avenger*, he initially refused to distribute the spoils until they were all together again, but after a month had passed with no word, the authorities considered *The Avenger* to be lost. Captain King was then obligated to divide the shares between those who had made it back while an official news release to the colonies carried the word the that the naval hero, Captain Jack Read, had been declared dead, killed in action off the Spanish Main.

14. Impenetrable

Mary's inability to convince anyone in her family that slavery was inherently wrong taught her a valuable lesson, the necessity of sucking up her emotions and keeping them to herself. Emotional displays were equated with weakness in this civilized world, doubly so for women, so if anyone was to take her seriously, she must always present them with a stoic exterior. She also began to develop a better understanding of her mother, her coping skills, and how she always seemed so even keeled no matter what the circumstances might be.

It was Mary's pragmatic approach to the world that finally helped her deal with the concept of slavery. While never doubting it was an injustice, she developed the attitude that the abolition of slavery was not up to well-meaning people like her, but up to the slaves themselves to stand up and tell the world that they were humans, too. The majority of slaves in South Carolina knew all about the small groups of runaways that had made their way to Florida where they had been given both freedom and land. The Spanish, looking to cause unrest within the English colonies as part of the war effort, had issued a proclamation and were actively promoting that any slave who deserted to St Augustine would be given the same treatment, so the solution to slavery was really quite clear. If enough slaves chose this option, then slavery would disappear, and plantation owners would be required to pay human beings for their expertise and labor. The rice would still grow and be harvested, but it would have to be sold for a higher price, and the plantation owners would make less money. So what?

On the other hand, if the slaves chose to accept their roles and remain beholden to their masters, then they were complicit in the concept of slavery, and their lot in life was their own fault. Mary had resolved her problem with slavery by recognizing that slaves, like all human beings, possessed the power of free will.

Mary became so adept at presenting an impenetrable front that when the news of Jack's death reached the plantation she didn't show so much as a public flinch. She simply commented how proud she was to have known the man who turned from pirate to a king's man and died a hero's death. No one would ever be witness to her emotional devastation and hours of inconsolable tears that preceded her sleep for the weeks that followed. During each day she was Joseph's perfect second hand and discharged her duties with clockwork efficiency. She spoke to Jethro on an almost daily basis and had become quite comfortable again with viewing him as a valuable plantation commodity.

Jack's death was bittersweet for Anne. The knowledge that he would not be showing up ensured that she would never have to disclose to Mary what she had learned about the marriage laws, but she had also liked Jack. How could she not? He was the image of his father, the man she had adored.

Anne, perhaps singularly, understood the transformation that had occurred in her daughter, and the common ground she and Mary shared served to further cement their rather unique bond. It also gave Anne the ability to see through Mary's exterior facade and appreciate the necessity of her private grieving beneath. Anne, therefore, waited for more than a month after news of Jack's death before bringing up the delicate subject that Mary was about to turn thirty years old, and to secure her future happiness, she should consider finding a husband.

"Do you honestly think after my time with Jack, that I could actually settle for one of the pompous, arrogant, so called gentlemen that they have here in the colonies?" Mary was incredulous.

"I settled with Joseph, and things haven't gone all that badly for me, have they? Besides, you're in a position to select someone you actually want. In my case I had no choice; my father pre-selected Joseph for me and married me off to him as soon as he got me off the boat."

"I really think I'd rather stay here, run the plantation and end up being an old maid rather than becoming a frustrated wife running a house. This way I will retain my freedoms."

"What about companionship in your old age?"

"I've known passion in my life, and I dare say that's more than most wives around here can say."

"I can probably grant you that," Anne smiled knowingly. Here was something else that she and her daughter had in common. "But you are still a young woman."

"I'm confident that my memories will sustain me well into old age."

"But you've got so many years ahead of you, Mary. What if you could find that passion again?"

"Here?" Mary shook her head. "The men around here treat ladies as if they are going to break. The only passion towards women any of them have appears to be for their slave girls."

"Mary!" Anne admonished.

"Oh you know it's true, mother. Everyone just turns a blind eye and nobody ever mentions it."

"All the same," Anne quickly returned the discussion to topic at hand. "What harm would come of at least letting suitors call on you? You may meet someone nice, someone you like."

"I wouldn't get your hopes up. Jack is dead."

"But you are not. Jack lived life to the fullest; I can't imagine he would want you to spend the rest of yours without at least trying."

Mary fell silent for a full minute and then swallowed hard; her mother was probably right. She sat contemplatively looking at her hands, took in a deep breath, slowly exhaled and looked up. "All right, mother," she relented. "I'll see suitors if they would care to call, but I'm not committing to actually doing anything." She looked deliberately into her mother's eyes. "Agreed?"

"Agreed, you have complete control." Anne nodded. "And don't worry; I'll take care of everything. I'll put the word out to Charleston society that only the most eligible of gentleman may call on Miss Mary Burleigh."

Jeremy Cartwright, the first gentleman to call, was a wealthy widower with no children and only five years older than Mary. He was a handsome man, dressed in the finest European silk, who made a grand entrance riding up to the house on an impressive black stallion. Mary greeted him in the drawing room.

"Where do you live, Mr. Cartwright?" Mary asked politely.

"I have a rice plantation in the south and a town house in Charleston," he replied. "I alternate between them."

"Do you also have business dealings in Charleston, then?"

"Just my club, but" He looked quizzical. "I must say, I find it rather odd, Miss Burleigh, that you should be inquiring about my business affairs."

"Really, why is that?"

"Well, ladies don't have much interest in business, do they?' He was annoyingly matter of fact.

"I'll have you know, sir, that I take quite a role in the management of this plantation and I have been on several trading tips to the Caribbean." Mary controlled her voice, matching his mannerisms.

"Well, I am sure that once you are married you wouldn't have to be concerned about those sorts of things."

"What sorts of things would a married lady do, then?" Mary forced herself to remain polite by concentrating on keeping her hands in her lap.

"A proper plantation owner's wife runs the household and manages the domestic slaves."

"I see." She was beginning to understand all too well. "And would these wifely duties extend to also including management of the town house?"

"Of course not," he laughed. It was a belittling laugh. "The town house is a gentleman's retreat. No, when you're my wife, you'll stay on the plantation and just take care of the main house."

"Don't you feel you are being rather presumptuous, Mr. Cartwright."

"Excuse me, Miss Burleigh, but I was under the impression that you were looking for a husband."

"I am hoping to meet a compatible gentleman, yes."

"Then I would be expecting you to be rather more anxious than you appear to be, even grateful that I am here calling at all. You're not going to find many widowers as young as me, and let's face it; you're already too old for a man who would be in the market for a first wife."

Without expression, Mary leaned forward and picked up and rang a small bell that was sitting on the table in front of her, deliberately placed it back on the table, and then slowly rose to her feet. "Thank you for stopping by Mr. Cartwright," she said as one of the house slaves entered the room. "I believe we are all finished here. Bessie," She said, turning to look at the attentive slave. "You may show this gentleman out."

"Suit yourself, Miss Burleigh." Mr. Cartwright responded in a most ungentlemanly manner. "But with your attitude you're going to be ending up a spinster, and you'll be spending your days wishing you'd grabbed me when you could."

"Goodbye Mr. Cartwright." Mary turned away and stared at the garden through the bay window. Nothing more needed to be said. She continued looking at the flowers outside until Anne came into the room, then quickly turned around and flopped down onto the couch.

"From his expression as he was leaving," Anne said as she settled into the chair opposite. "I'm assuming things did not go very well with Jeremy Cartwright."

"He was the epitome of arrogance, mother. I found him an insulting bore." Mary's whole body convulsed into a shiver. "This man wasn't looking for a wife for companionship; all he wanted was someone to take care of his plantation house while he went whoring in Charleston." She let her head fall back and spoke to the ceiling. "Do I really have to continue this charade?"

Anne leaned forward and took her daughter's hands in hers. "Don't worry, Mary," she said reassuringly. "I'm confident that Mr. Cartwright wasn't representative of men at large. Keep your chin up and give this process a chance."

For the remainder of that spring and well into summer, suitors continued to call on Mary, and while she admitted that a couple of them were pleasant, she showed no interest in having any of them return. The finest of South Carolina's eligible men with their wealth, good looks, and impeccable manners all had the same overwhelming negative against them: they were not Jack. But then Charles came by.

Charles Adams was a man of Mary's age with a slender frame and receding hairline. He was not unattractive, but certainly not handsome either. He stood less than an inch taller than Mary and appeared to be slightly uncomfortable in his well-tailored suit and shiny riding boots, probably because they were new.

Every man who had called on Mary to this point had started the conversation with the same bravado touting their wealth and property, but Charles instead began by asking questions about her. He was the first person to seem genuinely interested in Mary as a person, and she almost immediately felt drawn to his warm nature.

"So tell me, Mr. Adams, what is it that you do?" Mary finally asked him because, this time, she actually wanted to hear about it.

"I would be honored, Miss Burleigh, it you would call me Charles."

"But of course. And please, my name is Mary."

"Thank you Mary. To answer your question, my family grows indigo at an estate to the north of here. Our property is by no means as magnificent as yours, but we are a growing enterprise."

"Isn't indigo still an experimental crop in this part of the world?" Mary cocked her head inquisitively.

"It was," he replied with happy surprise. "I am impressed that you have even heard about the indigo trade from the colonies."

"It is something my father and I looked into when we heard that an indigo plantation could earn ten times the revenue of tobacco and five times that of rice, but we learned that the plants do not develop well in the Carolinas."

"We were fortunate to be able to buy some seed from Eliza Pickney who has developed the ideal strain for growing indigo here, and it is proving to be most successful for us. Our last shipment to England resulted in a substantial profit." His enthusiasm made him sit taller. "So much so, that I am now able to be bold enough to ask to come here make your acquaintance." He leaned forward and took a drink of tea. "Until recently our family did not have much money, which explains why I am still unmarried at thirty years old."

Mary liked Charles because he was down to earth and enterprising, and like her, he was actively involved in managing his family estate instead of being content to let overseers run things. On his second visit she learned that he had no interest in city life, and his desire for a wife was due to a genuine search for companionship. However, after his third visit, Mary concluded that companion was perhaps the nicest word she could use to describe Charles to herself. He would, indeed, make a very fine companion and she had no doubt that he would include his future wife in all aspects of his life. Other than towards his business, though, he seemed rather devoid of passion. True, Mary would have no worries about Charles cavorting with his slaves, but it would be comforting if she knew that he at least thought about such things. Still, as her mother kept telling her, good companionship was going to be that much more important to her at some point later in life.

15. Jury Rigging

"Break out the rum, double rations for everybody," Jack called out as the crew of *The Avenger* gathered in front of him and stood amongst the debris strewed across their battle damaged deck. They had drifted to a safe distance away from the payroll ship before setting her afire and were now more than ready for a celebratory drink while watching the blazing enemy vessel disappear beneath the waves. It had been a hard won victory. While death in action had always been a possibility, this was the first time under Jack's command that anyone had actually been lost. The mugs of rum went down as quickly as the Spanish ship.

As soon as the payroll vessel had completely gone under, Jack drained the remaining drops from his drink and tossed his mug aside. "All right then, lads," he said. "Here's our situation. With the top half of our mast blown off and down here on the deck," he hoisted his left foot up onto the timber for emphasis, "and the rest of our rig shot up like it is," he pointed up towards a ripped piece of mainsail that was fluttering noisily above him, "right now, we're dead in the water. The good news is that there's no damage to our hull, but even with the best jury rigging that we can do while we're at sea, the only direction we can hope to go is pretty much with the wind. There's a good easterly blowing, so that means we've no choice but to go west, and that heading is going to take us right into the Spanish Main." He looked over the sudden concern on the faces of his crew and then burst into a grin. "But since we really don't want to go there, we are fortunate to have a bit of luck on our side." He slowly raised his left hand and pointed his index finger south. "There are a small group of islands called the San Blas a bit southwest of where we are now between us and the mainland. If we can manage to get to one of them and run the Avenger up onto a beach, we can secure her steady enough to maybe lash the mast back up."

"Ain't there gonna to be Spanish at San Blas, cap'n?" Jermy's question was the obvious one, and the crew hushed to hear the answer.

"Most likely not," Jack responded assuredly. "These islands have no fresh water or strategic significance so there's no reason for a naval vessel to be there." He smiled at his crew as their concern melted from their weather beaten faces. "Well then, gentlemen." He spread his arms. "I suggest that it's time we get to work and see about getting' us under weigh." He looked up. "It looks to me like we still have about 20, maybe 25, feet of mast still left standing. Someone get up there, secure two blocks to the top, and run a halyard up one so we can hoist a short mainsail. The other one can carry a line to the bowsprit for us to set up a good sized jib on starboard. That'll give us plenty of sail to carry us downwind with a southerly drift." Jack spun around. "Helm," he shouted out. "Get us on a bearing of west sou'west as soon as we get moving."

Jack and the bosun spent hours on deck studying maps and using a sextant every night for the next two weeks as *The Avenger* maintained a slow southwesterly heading, and Jack finally assembled the crew. "We've been on course for fifteen days now," He announced. "And according to the stars, San Blas should be dead ahead sometime in the next day or so. I want all hands to keep a sharp eye, these islands lie low."

The entire crew gave up sleep to keep an active watch that night for fear that they might unknowingly sail past the low lying islands and into the clutches of the Spanish beyond. The light from the almost full moon in a cloudless sky was reassuring, but even in full daylight if they were a few miles too far north, they would have never seen them. It was only when someone yelled, "Land ho off the port bow," that following midday that any of them felt at ease.

Jack studied the closest island through his spyglass. "There's a fringe reef, but it's only on the windward side," he called out as he watched the waves breaking 200 feet or so from the shore. "Take us in closer to the north of it; it looks like there's a good beach there. Measurers to the bow and call it out."

Normally a ship would take in sail to slow down when approaching an unknown destination, but these were not normal circumstances. Since they were not in a position to be able to wait for high tide in order to beach *The Avenger*, they were going to need as much speed as they could summon. A risky strategy, but they were forced to run the risk between success and either foundering or overshooting the beach. In the condition *The Avenger* was in, they would not be able to turn her around.

The measurers alternated in calling out the depths from either side of the ship, and as soon as Jack was confident that he could see that the waves were making it all the way to the beach before breaking, he called to the helm for hard to port. The entire crew braced for impact, and the ship slid straight up onto the beach and lurched to a stop. Lines were immediately thrown over both sides, and crewmembers scampered ashore carrying stakes and mallets while the makeshift sails were dropped unceremoniously onto the deck.

Once the Avenger was secured to the beach Jack grabbed the main halyard, wrapped it five times around the middle of the top part of the mast which still lying on the deck where it had fallen during the battle, tied it off, and called for it to be hoisted up on end. It took the efforts of the entire crew to stand it upright next to the remaining stump and then lash the two parts together so it was held secure. By the end of the day the ship was fully rigged again, and the holes in the repairable sails had been sewed. "Almost as good as before," Jack proudly complemented his crew as he stared up the mast, then added, "except, of course, that it's about 30 feet shorter," which brought about raucous laughter throughout the ship's company underscoring the relief they all felt knowing that they now had a chance.

"Great work lads," Jack continued. "We'll spend the night here, get a well-earned rest, and leave with tomorrow's high tide. Sleep on shore if you like, but no fires. We don't want to attract any attention."

The next midday fully rested crewmembers were waist deep in the water untying the lines enabling *The Avenger* to right with the incoming tide. Lines were tied to the stern, and two rowboats pulled her out until she was a safe enough distance from the beach to not drift back into it. The crew then assembled on deck, eager to get under weigh and waiting for Jack to give them their heading.

"Do we sail north, captain?"

"No, we're heading east," Jack told them. That brought wide eyes to the crew. "Since the Spanish have undoubtedly sent a warship or two from Cuba by now, our best bet to avoid them is to beat a course towards the Lesser Antilles."

"But what about getting us to Port Royal?"

Jack broke into a huge grin, reached out with his right hand, and grabbed onto a stay as the ship slowly rocked side to side. "It's like this, lads," he explained. "If we report to Port Royal we'll have to share our gold with King George. Gold that each and every one of you have paid dearly for." He paused to enjoy the collective look of confusion. "Our Navy will most likely have written us off by now so they aren't expecting us. In fact, they won't even be looking for us, so why would we want to go showing up there and then giving them half of our gold? And we do have all the gold, you know. The two chests that *Rumrunner* took back to Jamaica with them were filled with just silver. I figured half of that would be a fair share for King George. We might be willing share the pieces of eight we took, lads, but we're keeping the doubloons for ourselves."

The crew was obviously pleased, but there was still concern and their cheers quickly subsided so Jack could continue.

"So, you see," He said jubilantly. "I don't plan for us to go to Jamaica. I promised I'd make you rich and get you back home. Well, we're all rich now, so shouldn't our destination be Gran Baha? If we follow the Windward Islands north into the Atlantic, we'll have a straight shot home through the Mayaguana Passage." He deeply inhaled the salt air in front of the boisterously cheering crew, then shouted out his order to unfurl the sails.

It was close to another month before *The Avenger* made it back to Gran Baha, fortunately managing to avoid any encounters along the way. Jack was delighted to see *Rumrunner* at anchor in the calm bay as they sailed past Gold Rock, and beyond it the beach was filling with people waving and cheering. Boats pushed out to greet them before they even had their sails furled, and once they dropped anchor men rushed gleefully ashore to reunite with their overjoyed families.

Jack, with two chests of gold next to his feet, sat in his dinghy grinning as his mother and Richard rushed to the shoreline to welcome him back. His mother locked onto Jack with an embrace that almost cut off his breath as soon as he stepped onto the beach, then held him at arm's length, her trembling hands gripping his shoulders and stared into his face. "You did it, Jack," she shouted excitedly. "I thought to never see you again, but well, you bloody well went and did it. Ahh, your father would be so proud." She pulled Jack towards herself again, this time giving him the opportunity to return the hug.

"*Rumrunner* looks to be in top shape, Richard," Jack said, nodding towards the sea.

"Aye, she is that, Jack. The naval shipyard does a good job in that regard." Richard chuckled. "Charged us for it, of course; but it was well worth it."

"Well, *The Avenger* needs a lot of work, so how about using *Rumrunner* to take me up to Charleston?" Jack's eyes flitted between both of their glares. "Don't give me that look. In case you're forgetting, for me the whole reason for this bloody venture of getting rich was so I could go and get Mary back."

"Think about it, Jack," Mary Read began, but he cut her off.

"What do you mean, 'think about it?' I haven't thought of anything else since we left." Jack was ready to begin a rampage, but his mother responded with characteristic matriarchal admonishment. "You just got here," she said calmly. "We will talk about it later."

Later came that night as Jack sat with his mug of rum staring at the celebratory bonfires as they lit up the beach. His mother eased down next to him. "Let's not fight, Jack, but please listen to me. Mary is probably already married, and seeing you would only bring heartbreak for the both of you. And even if she isn't, do you really believe you can fit into her world of high society and slavery?"

"I most likely will have more money than many of these so called society types, so I'm sure I'll have no trouble buying my way in." Jack was being polite, but doing so through guarded, clenched teeth.

"Takes more than money to be a gentleman, Jack," Mary Read smiled and nodded her head. She was annoyingly right. "Will you be buying a plantation, then?" He queried. "Gonna have slaves too, are you?"

Jack's slowly turned his head to latch his wide, unblinking eyes onto his mother's face. "No," he growled. "I don't know what I'll be doing, but it won't be that."

"But Mary's a plantation girl, Jack."

"Then I'll have to talk to her about it, won't I." He drained his rum and took a deep breath. "I love her, mother. I have to try." His voice was almost pleading. "I'm going to do this, and there isn't anything you can do or say to stop me. If she rejects me, so be it, but I have to give it a shot. I have to know. Please understand."

A week later *Rumrunner* sailed for Charleston with not only Jack, but also most of the inhabitants, men, women and children of Gold

Rock, aboard, eager to spend some of their riches in the stores and marketplaces and indulge for a while in life in the opulent hotels of the big city. Nobody would question their wealth because the conflict with Spain had ended, and colonial cities up and down the eastern seaboard had eagerly prepared for the returning war heroes and the riches they would be bringing with them.

Mary Read chose to remain behind, but did entrust Richard King with a shopping list. She also tasked him with staying close to her son.

16. The Suitor

"I see you're out in the summer sun without your hat on again, eh, Mary?" Joseph Burleigh teased as he strolled up behind his daughter. Mary had been leaning dreamily against the fence surrounding their newest rice field, mesmerized as she watched the tops of the tall green plants gently swaying in the afternoon breeze, but was now snapped back. "Hello father," she responded without moving from the fence, and then slowly turned to him as he settled against it next to her. "You won't tell mother, will you?"

"I suppose not, but the fact you're not losing that tan on your face rather gives you away anyhow. She frets about you not having the lily complexion that is more suited to a lady, you know. She really would prefer that you become more aware about how you appear in public."

"But I am aware," Mary chuckled brightly. "So much so that if a man were to choose not to speak to me because of my skin tone, then I am grateful to have my tan, for clearly, he would be a bore."

"Ah, that brings up the reason I came looking for you."

"Oh no," Mary dreaded hearing what she knew her father had come to say.

"Oh, yes. Your friend, Charles, has asked for a meeting with me."

"He's hardly a friend, Father." Mary turned back to looking at the rice. "I've only met the man three times."

"A suitor then," Joseph said brusquely, but instantly softened. "I stand corrected. But regardless, it follows that he intends to ask me for your hand."

"It all seems so business-like, doesn't it?" Mary sniffed as she stood upright and turned to face her father. "Does he suppose that I am a negotiable commodity, or perhaps a piece of property available for purchase?" She was clearly agitated.

"Settle down, Mary. I am quite certain he thinks nothing of the sort. He is simply following societal protocol, and you know that."

"I know, Father." Mary made no attempt to hide her frustration. "It's just that, he's..."

"He's what?"

"Oh, I don't know. Conventional, predictable, ordinary..."

"But you must like him. You did permit him to return twice which clearly suggests that you believe him to have at least some endearing qualities."

"I do like him, Father. He is a genuinely nice man and isn't all full of himself." Mary looked at her feet and became thoughtful. Charles would be an ideal husband if her goal were to settle down to the life of a proper lady. She couldn't really tell her father that her concern was that she didn't expect him to be exciting enough for her. Mary slowly raised her chin again and her forehead tightened. "So, what did you tell him? Did you grant Charles a meeting?"

"I haven't as yet given him any answer because I wanted to discuss it with you first. He comes from a good family and is clearly a respectable gentleman. He is also the only man whom you have deemed worthy to see more than once, so you might say you have created certain expectations." He quickly raised flats of both hands as Mary's scowling face snapped his way. "But," he maintained his pose of surrender. "I will not give my consent if you do not wish to marry him. That decision is all yours."

Mary's expression melted, and she threw her arms around Joseph. "Thank you, Father," her whisper exuded relief. "Would you, um, mind waiting just a few days before you do answer him," she added coyly.

Joseph took Mary's chin in his right hand and eased her face up to his. She was unable to conceal a wry smile. "All right, Mary. Tell me what is going on with you."

"It may be nothing, but a curious message was delivered to me yesterday from a wealthy gentleman by the name of Jed Carak, newly arrived in Charleston and seeking to find a wife and settle down. The messenger handed me Mr. Carak's card and asked if the gentleman may call on me tomorrow. It was so mysterious that I just had to agree."

"And I take it that since he may not be 'ordinary' you wish to hold off on Charles in case this Jed Carak catches your fancy?"

"Oh, you so understand, Father," Mary beamed.

"And yet you know nothing about him, other than he is a gentleman of wealth?"

"Maybe he's a privateer captain," Mary said wistfully. "An adventurer who's come here to spend the Spanish gold he acquired during the war and is seeking a likeminded woman to enjoy the good life with him."

Stifling his first reaction to blurt out, Joseph instead sported a sideways grin. "You truly have a wicked sense of humor, young lady. You almost had me there." He broke into a raucous guffaw. "Oh Mary," he brought his laughter under control and became serious again. "Please don't be expecting to be seeing any men like that anywhere in the colonies."

"No?" Mary forced curiosity to conceal her disappointment.

"No, I'm afraid not. Those type of men have gone back to their old pirate ways and they're about to play havoc with honest trade again. Fortunately, now that the war is over, his majesty will be able to free up some warships to keep The Bahamas safe for us."

Had this request for an audience from a mysterious last minute suitor not arrived, Mary would have blithely gone along with accepting the marriage proposal from Charles and mindlessly nodded "all right" when her father had approached her. Accepting that no one could compare to Jack and yielding to the diligent prompting of her mother and sisters, Mary had allowed herself to be eased into the expectations and conventions of life in South Carolina over the preceding months. This single incident, however, had re-awoken her awareness that there was still life beyond that. This meeting might not lead to anything at all. In fact, Mary had no expectation that it would, but she was welcoming the opportunity to take one last look at a potential alternative before making the final commitment to settle down. Charles wouldn't be hurt by having to wait a couple of days longer.

Mary sat demurely on the couch in the drawing room waiting for her suitor to be shown in, straining to listen to the muffled conversation in the hallway outside. Rather than wearing a bulky formal greeting dress, it was too warm of a day for that, she was dressed in a light summer frock which matched the orange and yellow flowers in the large vase on the coffee table. Plus, since first impressions count, she didn't want to be taken for just another colonial lady. It was also her intention to initially present a rather aloof demeanor to her caller.

The door opened and she prepared to greet her caller with a very formal, "Hello, Mr. Carak, but as he stepped into the room, her mouth involuntarily opened and the question, "Jack?" fell out of it. Suddenly abandoning all form of protocol, she leaped to her feet and rushed across the room repeatedly screaming, "Jack, Jack." Unable to summon the stoicism that had served her so well since her return to South Carolina, Mary had no control over her overwhelming surge of emotion and unabashedly ignored the tears of happiness flowing down her cheeks. She collapsed forward into Jack's welcoming arms for comfort. The use of words eluded them both, they were simply content to hold onto each other, but as soon as Mary found composure, she stepped back slightly so she could look up at Jack's face. It really was him.

Since Mary's screams had reverberated through the house, Anne was compelled to intrude and burst into the room. As soon as she saw who the man was who was holding her daughter, her hand froze tightly onto the doorknob and she, also overwhelmed at the surprise, momentarily lost her voice.

"Look, mother." Mary bubbled excitedly. "It's Jack. It really is Jack."

"So I see." Anne quickly recovered, released the doorknob, and walked towards them.

"I took heed of the advice you gave me on Gran Baha, Mrs. Burleigh," Jack said proudly with his hand clasped to Mary's waist. "And I stand before you now as a man with the requisite wealth to woo your daughter." Arm still around Mary, he turned to look her. "Did you pick up on my pseudonym?" He asked.

Mary tried to answer that she had not, but all that came out of her mouth was breath.

"I was afraid you wouldn't see me if you knew who I was," Jack admitted. "And I couldn't abide not seeing you, even if it meant having you reject me. I can't tell you how thrilled I was when we landed in Charleston and heard that you were accepting suitors. That you were not yet married."

"We were told you were dead, Jack." Anne's voice was questioning. "There was an official naval report that you had died at the hands of the Spanish."

"I assure you I am very much alive." Even his eyes were smiling. "But it might be best for all concerned that certain people, especially the navy, continue to believe otherwise."

"Tell us what happened?" Anne insisted. "Please, let's sit down."

Jack eased Mary to the couch, sat down next to her, and held her hands in his as he told the two women about the adventure he and his crew had endured. "You see," he said when he had finished his story. "I understood why you left, Mary. As a poor pirate I couldn't give you the life you were accustomed to. But your mother," he smiled over at Ann, "Told me that I could qualify if I took the king's marque and made my fortune. So, now that I am rich, I can present myself as a proper gentleman in hopes that you will have me now."

"But what about your island home, Jack? What of the sea?" Mary spoke through an open mouthed smile, her head dancing excitedly.

"For you, Mary, I'm happy to forgo all of that. I'll buy you the biggest house in Charleston, or a country estate, or whatever you want. Whatever it is that will make you happy."

"You've impressed me, Jack." Anne interrupted, denying Mary the opportunity to respond to him further. "And your arrival here like this has not only been thrilling, but it is also quite overwhelming, to say the least. Would it be too much of an imposition to ask you to return again tomorrow? And, as you can imagine, Mary and I have many things that we need to discuss now that we know that you are not only alive, but here."

"But of course." Jack rose to his feet.

"Shall we say early afternoon?" Anne insisted on dominating the conversation and nervously watched Jack and Mary smiling at each other while he added, "Until tomorrow, then."

17. Truth

It didn't take long after Jack had left that the house became abuzz with the news that Mary's "pirate captain turned war hero" had come for her. Everybody was anxious to meet him, and it was simply assumed, without Mary even saying anything, that she and Jack were about to be married. Suddenly feeling confined and in desperate need of time alone, Mary excused herself from her exuberant sisters, who were already discussing the wedding plans without her, and went outside for air. In case anyone would think to follow, she immediately stepped down from the porch and quickly ran away from the house, maintaining a sufficiently brisk pace to ensure that no-one would be able to keep up with her until she was well into the countryside and could breathe freely again. She plopped herself down in a very unladylike manner at the base of a gnarled old willow tree, her childhood favorite place, leaned against the trunk with her hands around her knees, and stared up into the protective cover of branches. Jack appearing at this opportune time was the best thing that could have ever happed to her, but something was clearly wrong. Her mother had prevented the two of them from being alone and maintained rigid control over the conversation while he was at the house. Anne should have been happy and eminently supportive, ideally leaving them together to talk, but her actions clearly demonstrated that she did not want Jack to propose. "Why?" Mary demanded of the willow, but the leaves simply rustled calmly as they always had. She closed her eyes, pushed her chin against her chest, and slowly rocked back and forth while her brain attempted to muddle through what was going on.

The comforting solitude lasted for almost an hour, and Mary would have remained in that state even longer but was disturbed when she sensed movement in front of her and was obliged to slowly raise her head to see who it was. It was her father.

"May I join you?" Joseph sat on the ground next to her without waiting for a reply. "I thought I might find you here. You used to call this your thinking tree." He slid his left arm around Mary's shoulders and gently eased her towards him as she turned to rest her head against him. "So your mystery suitor turned out to be exactly what you had hoped for." He kissed the top of her head and then added, "Even more so."

"I was so thrilled when I saw it was Jack," Mary cooed. "Jack, alive and come for me." She snuggled up against her father.

"Yes, about that." Joseph's jovial voice assured Mary that she had no need for concern. "It appears that your Jack has an abysmal sense of protocol. Your mother thought he might actually ask you to marry him right then and there without even consulting me first."

Mary's eyes slowly moved up to take in her father's smiling face. Was that it? Could that have been the reason that Anne had so deliberately shut Jack down? "I do want to marry him, Father," she told him.

"Well, of course you do Mary." Joseph chuckled. "But may I at least meet the fellow first? A little semblance of decorum would be nice." Joseph stood up and eased his daughter to her feet next to him.

"Yes, of course, Father. You should be in the room with me when Jack returns tomorrow." Mary nodded as she spoke and then threw her arms around Joseph's neck. "Thank you, thank you; I just know that you are going to like him."

Anne was unable to sleep that night and sat outside on the front porch staring up at the stars. She dreaded breaking Mary's heart, but knew that she had no choice in the matter. Furthermore, she must have this conversation with her daughter before Jack returned. The coming morning meant telling Mary that her interpretation of the marriage laws had been wrong and that half siblings were absolutely forbidden to marry. When Jack inevitably proposes tomorrow, Mary was not only going to have to reject him, but it would also be the right thing for her to do to tell him the real reason why.

In spite of her agitated thoughts, Ann must have dozed for a while because it was too soon that the first light of dawn glowed on the horizon. Anne gasped in a deep breath, stood up and went inside the house.

Mary, understandably excited, arose early and was surprised to see her mother already sitting in the breakfast room when she entered. "Before you meet with Jack again, there is something I have to tell you." Anne blurted out quickly, not allowing Mary to speak or even wishing her daughter a good morning first. Certainly, this was not destined to be a good morning. "There is something you need to know."

"Oh, I already spoke to father." Mary replied lightly. "And everything is all right; he is going to be with me when Jack comes by so the two of them can meet."

"That isn't what I need to talk to you about." Anne's voice was monotone. "Sit down, Mary."

"If this is anything against my marrying Jack, Mother, don't bother yourself." Mary instantly went on the defensive as she lowered her bottom onto the edge of a chair. "There isn't a thing you're going to be able to say that will make me not want him."

"Believe me, Mary, when I tell you that I really like Jack, and I know the two of you are a perfect match, but," Anne took a breath and looked hard at Mary, silently studying her daughter's face as if she had never seen it before. Then, instead of continuing with her overly well-rehearsed speech, she cocked her head to the left and her mouth slid into an involuntary half smile. "You have earlobes," Ann announced, her solemn voice suddenly giving way to obvious excitement.

"I beg your pardon." Mary almost choked.

"Earlobes. Mary, you have earlobes."

"Perhaps you haven't noticed, Mother, but everyone in the family except you has them. It's hardly something to become excited about." Mary's voice shifted from confused to annoyed. "And what on earth could earlobes possibly have to do with Jack?"

"Absolutely everything!" Anne leaped to her feel and clamped her hands onto Mary's shoulders. "You see," Anne's head vibrated from side to side. "Calico Jack didn't have earlobes either."

"Which means?" Mary shrugged free of her mother's hands and leaned back into the chair.

"It means that Jack Rackham wasn't your father."

"And?" This was becoming tiresome. What was it that her mother was not telling her?

"Jack is not your half-brother at all."

"But what bearing does that have on anything?" Mary's head waved from side to side in frustration. "We know that half siblings are free to marry."

"No," Anne snapped and stood erect. "No, they are not."

"What?"

Anne sat down. "After you concluded that they were, I checked into it further just to be sure and found out that half siblings are considered the same as regular brothers and sisters." Her mouth twitched as she took in Mary's 'why didn't you tell me' glare. "I couldn't bear to see you unhappy again, Mary." Anne answered the look calmly, but then fell into an uncharacteristic display of emotion. "I never expected Jack to show up here, so I felt it best to just keep it from you." Her trembling hands grabbed Mary's. "I'm so sorry."

One look at Anne's genuine tear filled eyes defused Mary's anger. Withholding information that could unnecessarily upset a loved one was, after all, an act of kindness. An act that she, herself, had committed by securing Jack's mother's silence about what appeared to be the true nature of her and Jack's relationship. She gave her mother's hands a quick squeeze. "Does that mean I really am your husband's daughter, then?"

"Umm, actually, no, you are not."

"Then you had better explain, mother." Mary sat bolt upright and stared directly at Anne.

"You are the daughter of a pirate, just not Jack Rackham." Anne's embarrassment underscored that she had been unprepared to face this turn in their conversation, but she also welcomed the opportunity to finally tell someone the truth. "Your father's name was Chris Condent; he was another pirate who was also getting restless back then in Nassau. Mary introduced us. He became the quartermaster on the William, the ship we commandeered to go pirating with. When we first started out, I was with Chris and Mary was with Jack Rackham.

After we'd captured our first ship, Calico Jack made Chris the captain of it, and Chris immediately wanted to go and take it pirating off the coast of Africa. He was concerned that we were going to be hunted down if we remained in the Bahamas. He really wanted me to go with him."

"But you didn't want to?"

"No." Anne looked down and her face glowed crimson. "You have to know that I really liked Chris, he was a brave and handsome and a good man to be with, but," she bit her lower lip. "I was in love with Calico Jack. I knew that if Chris went away, then Mary would be willing to share Jack with me again, just like she did before, so when Chris left for Africa, I chose to stay with them on the William."

Mary was smiling. Her own mother, this was unbelievable.

"So there we were," Anne continued. "Mary and I were both sharing Jack. I'll admit to being jealous when it came out first that Mary was carrying his baby, but I never said anything. They wouldn't have understood, and it would have ruined everything." Anne smiled at Mary. "Even if had considered that Chris might have actually been your father, I would have just dismissed it, not wanting it to be so, and over time I never had any doubt at all that you were Jack's.

So, when you figured it out that Jack was your brother and Mary Read was there to confirm it that was the truth, it didn't even occur to me to suggest that he might not be. By then I had completely forgotten about the time I was with Chris. But, even if I had remembered and said something right then and there, I couldn't have been sure so it wouldn't have made any difference. Would it?"

"But you are sure about it now?" Mary asked earnestly.

"Absolutely," Anne chuckled as she recollected. "I can remember now how I used to tease Chris about his earlobes because I don't have any, and neither did Calico Jack. The only way you could have them is by being Chris Condent's daughter, because he was the only other man I had been with."

"So Jack and I are not brother and sister after all?" It felt good to say it.

"That is correct, which means that you and Jack are completely free to marry." Anne's turbulent range of emotion had been made more intense by her lack of sleep, and as she lunged forward to hug Mary she might even have been crying. "I can't tell you how happy I am, Mary. Jack is so much like his father; I can't imagine a better man in the world for you."

When Jack entered the drawing room that afternoon the only thing he saw was Mary standing next to a chair wearing the same blue dress that she was wearing when he first laid eyes on her. He began to move excitedly towards her, but then realized that her parents were sitting side by side on the couch to his right, so he immediately straightened up and slowed his gait. Joseph stood up and moved next to Mary, but Anne remained quietly seated.

"Jack," Mary said formally. "I would like you to meet my father, Joseph Burleigh." She turned slightly. "Father, may I present Captain Jack Read."

"It is an honor to meet you, sir," Jack extended his right hand and Joseph immediately clasped onto it for a solid handshake.

"I know it would be customary at this time to ask for your daughter's hand, sir," Jack said to him. "And I mean no disrespect. But Mary is a free spirit and should be making this decision completely on her own."

"I couldn't agree more, lad." Joseph broke into a wide grin, and he affixed his right hand to Jack's shoulder and looked directly into his eyes. "And any man who is able to win Mary's heart is certain to have my blessing." He stepped back and extended his left hand towards Anne who slid her right into it and quietly rose from the couch. "Come along, Anne," Joseph said. "It's time for us to give these two the opportunity to be alone."

Jack turned to Mary as soon as her parents had closed the door and enveloped her in his arms, following through on the desire he had kept contained since he had first entered the room. Her arms clasped around his neck, and her parted lips moved to meet his in the kiss they had both waited so long for, the sensual kiss of unbridled passion. "I love you Mary," Jack gasped as he briefly broke free. Still embracing, they descended onto the couch, and Jack looked intently into Mary's eyes. "Mary Burleigh," he said. "Will you marry me?"

Mary was barely able to utter, "Yes, of course," before their lips were once again together, and the subsequent who knows how long was spent in loving embrace without words.

They slowly pulled apart, adoringly gazing at each other, and Mary noticed the smirk on Jack's face. "What is it?" she asked.

"Your mother," Jack chuckled. "Today was the first time I have ever seen her not have the last word. In fact, she had no words at all."

"Ah, that is colonial convention for ladies. A wife must always act deferentially to her husband when in a public or formal setting. And a man coming to the house with a marriage proposal is most definitely a formal occasion.

"Do you think your father found me presumptuous?"

"I hope so; I wouldn't have you any other way." Mary reached for the bell. "Let me call for tea."

It only took ten minutes before there was a knock on the door, and Bessie came in carrying a tray. Mary watched Jack tense at the realization that he was going to have to contend with slavery, a part of everyday life here in the colonies. As the house slave closed the door behind her, Mary slid her hand reassuringly on top of Jack's. "I'll teach you the rationale I employed when I returned," she told him, then proceeded to pour tea into the fine china cups.

"You've really learned to come to terms with slavery again, then?" Jack was clearly disappointed.

"No," Mary handed him a cup and saucer. "But I was required to develop a means of self-deception in order to tolerate being here."

Jack thoughtfully sipped his tea, smiled, and then downed the entire cupful. "So, Mary," he placed the cup and saucer back on the table. "Where shall we live after we are married? As I said before, I have sufficient wealth for us to either live in town or a country mansion. I'll even buy you both if you would like." His smile suddenly flattened. "But I do have a caveat." His words were now being delivered almost as a warning. "Since I have no need of a source of income, we won't be buying a plantation. Don't worry; if you feel the need for house servants, I will employ a staff of free men and women for you. But we will never own a human."

"Do you really want to be in this world, Jack?"

"I want to be wherever you are happy, Mary, and this is your home."

"But I don't want to be here anymore, Jack." Mary scooped his hands into hers. "Don't you see, I adapted to it after I thought you were dead, but that adaptation was just stifling the person I really am. The person you awoke in me. That's who I want to be, and I can't be her in South Carolina." She ginned. "But I can be her at Gold Rock." She fell into his open arms. "Take me home, Jack.

Epilogue

The war with Spain and France had been costly for England, and now that it was over attention focused on the American colonies as a means to raise additional revenue to pay for it. British warships, now free to roam the eastern seaboard, enforced the previously all but ignored Molasses Act, and additional bills to raise taxes on the colonists' trade began to breed general discontent with England.

While Joseph Burleigh was generally correct, many of the privateers did return to lives of piracy after the war, the more entrepreneurial amongst them made their services available to the American colonists. Their fast ships enabled smuggled goods to be sold in the markets of Harbour Island, and molasses to flow into secret ports along the American coastline tax free. Such was the business arrangement that Jack made with Mary's father shortly after the wedding. Mary became the quartermaster on *The Avenger*, and business travel enabled the two of them to make frequent visits to her family.

Anne re-established and continued her friendship with Mary Read as the mothers-in-law, occasionally even visiting her at Gold Rock. Nobody else ever learned of her time as Anne Bonny, and she continued to maintain her image as a conservative lady. But she also enjoyed the old life vicariously through the exploits of her daughter.

THE END

About the Author

Ronald Haines finds the study of history and historical people fascinating. He believes that people are really no different now than they were even thousands of years ago in terms of their motivations, desires, prejudices and biases. Ronald's Historical Fiction novels are well researched for historical fact, and through his characters readers will be put inside the heads of the people who there, living it.

Ronald is an existential humanist: goal directed, self-motivated, and a big believer in individual freedom and its requisite companion, personal responsibility. You'll find these traits expressed throughout his works.

Ronald genuinely enjoys the process of writing and can be totally immersed in whatever world he is creating for hours at a time. But when not at his desk writing, you'll find him sailing, gardening, hiking through the woods, or walking along a beach.

Read more at https://ronaldhaines.com.

www.ingramcontent.com/pod-product-compliance
Lightning Source LLC
Chambersburg PA
CBHW071227260626
47162CB00004B/1452